**'There is anoth[er solution,' he said]
slowly. 'Come h[ome with me.']**

'With you? You're kidding.'

'I'm not.' Now that he'd offered, he realized how much he liked the idea. To a man who thrived on new experiences, this was certain to become a memorable occasion. 'I have a spare room.'

She lowered her voice. 'I can't stay at your house.'

'Why not?'

'You kissed me.'

'I'd do it again, if you'd let me, but kisses are a separate issue. I'm offering my house with no strings attached.'

She nibbled her lip. 'We won't cramp your style?'

'I wouldn't have offered if your presence would pose a problem,' he said quietly. It would, but the problem was with him, not her. He probably wouldn't close his eyes all night because of Megan lying in the other room on the spare double bed.

# A&E DRAMA

Blood pressure is high and pulses are racing in these fast-paced, dramatic stories from Mills & Boon® Medical Romance™. They'll move a mountain to save a life in an emergency, be they the crash team, ER doctors, fire, air or land rescue paramedics. There are lots of critical engagements amongst the high tensions and emotional passions in these exciting stories of lives and loves at risk!

**A&E DRAMA**

**Hearts are racing!**

# A WHITE KNIGHT IN ER

BY
JESSICA MATTHEWS

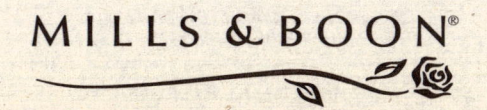

MILLS & BOON®

To Hospital personnel everywhere,
for the risks taken in service to others.

**DID YOU PURCHASE THIS BOOK WITHOUT A COVER?**
If you did, you should be aware it is **stolen property** as it was reported *unsold and destroyed* by a retailer. Neither the author nor the publisher has received any payment for this book.

*All the characters in this book have no existence outside the imagination of the author, and have no relation whatsoever to anyone bearing the same name or names. They are not even distantly inspired by any individual known or unknown to the author, and all the incidents are pure invention.*

*All Rights Reserved including the right of reproduction in whole or in part in any form. This edition is published by arrangement with Harlequin Enterprises II B.V. The text of this publication or any part thereof may not be reproduced or transmitted in any form or by any means, electronic or mechanical, including photocopying, recording, storage in an information retrieval system, or otherwise, without the written permission of the publisher.*

*This book is sold subject to the condition that it shall not, by way of trade or otherwise, be lent, resold, hired out or otherwise circulated without the prior consent of the publisher in any form of binding or cover other than that in which it is published and without a similar condition including this condition being imposed on the subsequent purchaser.*

*MILLS & BOON and MILLS & BOON with the Rose Device are registered trademarks of the publisher.*

*First published in Great Britain 2003*
*Harlequin Mills & Boon Limited,*
*Eton House, 18-24 Paradise Road, Richmond, Surrey TW9 1SR*

© Jessica Matthews 2003

ISBN 0 263 83461 1

*Set in Times Roman 10½ on 11½ pt.*
03-0803-49565

*Printed and bound in Spain*
*by Litografia Rosés, S.A., Barcelona*

# CHAPTER ONE

'WHERE is everybody?' Gene Webber placed several sheets of paper on top of the chest-high counter surrounding the nurses' station and glanced around the eerily quiet ER.

Megan Erickson looked up from the chart in front of her to smile at the red-haired twenty-six-year-old EMT who'd worked with her for the past several years. 'They usually disappear when there's a lull.'

'Well, if you see Dr Taylor, would you tell him that we got those results he wanted?' He tapped the pages on the counter.

'Sure. Do you know where he went?'

Gene shook his head. 'After Dr Fleming came, they both disappeared.'

'Dwight's here?' she asked, surprised that he hadn't stayed long enough to say hello like he usually did.

Gene shrugged. 'He walked in ten, fifteen minutes ago. He asked about you, but you were with Mrs Johnson. He ran into Dr Taylor and I haven't seen either of them since.'

'Well, they can't have strayed too far. Did Dwight leave a message?'

'Not that I know of,' Gene apologized. 'I can ask around if you want.'

'Don't bother. I'll see him later, I'm sure.' She smiled. 'He's probably getting advice on what to pack for his trip to Mexico.' Dwight had talked for the past six months about wanting to go on a medical missions tour and his month-long stint would start in less than two weeks. While she was glad that he was pursuing a dream of his, she wanted to think about weddings and combining households.

Between the death of her brother and his wife, and taking Angela and Trevor under her wing, she'd placed her own dreams on hold and was eager to get them back on track.

'Has Dr Taylor been to Mexico?'

'Where hasn't the man been?' she asked lightly. Dr Taylor had the staying power of a dandelion seed. A consortium of physicians staffed their ER and the man who was currently under contract had taken a leave of absence because of his wife's poor health. His substitute, Jonas Taylor, had arrived four weeks ago and would stay for three more months. After that, Stanton would become another listing on an already impressive résumé.

In spite of, or because of his varied experiences, he was a top-notch emergency physician. She couldn't have asked for someone better. The man was a veritable rock in a crisis.

He was also the most handsome guy she'd seen outside of a magazine.

Perhaps she shouldn't have noticed how Dwight's golden good looks paled in comparison to Jonas's dark coloring, but she had. Jonas's dark hair in a military-style cut should have made him seem stern and imposing, but the twinkle in his midnight-black eyes and his good-natured grin softened the impression. He admitted to loving the outdoors and his tanned skin corroborated his claim.

He was tall and lean, which was surprising considering the amount of food he put away. According to rumor, he'd taken part in nearly every sport or activity humanly possible and Megan guessed that he'd probably excelled at each one, too.

Jonas Taylor was definitely the most intriguing fellow to work in this ER since the founding fathers had built the hospital, but he wouldn't know commitment if it hung on his coattails. Other women might be only interested in having a good time but, with two children to consider, Megan wanted stability and someone to share the responsibility of raising them. She couldn't afford to think of anything else, no matter how exciting the prospect.

'He's been all over,' Gene admitted. 'I'd be happy if I'd visited a fourth of the places he's seen.'

'No kidding, but, then, what else is he going to spend his salary on?' She didn't know the exact details of his contract, but she knew the hospital had picked up the tab for his rent and utilities. His paycheck, minus Uncle Sam's cut for taxes, had to be nearly pure profit.

Gene sighed. 'Oh, to be so lucky.'

'Yeah, but remember—the grass is always greener on the other side of the fence.'

'Only because he can afford fertilizer,' he answered gloomily.

Megan giggled. 'Cheer up. Maybe the next lottery ticket you buy will pay off.'

'I can hope.' He glanced around the department once again. 'Do you mind if I run down to the cafeteria for a minute? I hear they baked a fresh batch of peanut-butter cookies and I want some before they disappear.'

Knowing Gene's weakness for peanut butter, Megan chuckled. 'Go ahead, but don't dawdle.'

'I won't. I'll even bring one back for you.'

'Make that two and I'll give you an extra five minutes.'

'You're on.'

He scampered away and she tried to focus on the chart in front of her, but couldn't. Dwight now occupied her thoughts and, sadly enough, those same thoughts were more troubling than satisfying.

Things weren't working out the way she'd expected.

She'd accepted Dwight's engagement ring a month before her brother and his wife had died in a boating accident, and with no other siblings to look after their two small children, she'd taken in her niece and nephew, Angela and

Trevor. The past year had been a time of adjustment for all of them, but she'd made the switch from doting aunt to mother of now four-year-old Angela and eighteen-month-old Trevor.

During that time, and at Dwight's suggestion, they'd postponed wedding plans until they'd settled into a new routine. At first, she'd been thrilled by his thoughtfulness, but as time had gone on and he'd appeared content to leave their future on the shelf, her confidence had begun to waver.

Those doubts had grown when she'd realized something else. After nearly a year, he acted as uncomfortable around the children as he had on the day they'd brought them from Iowa to her home in Nebraska. As far as she was concerned, he simply seemed to tolerate them, when she'd hoped he'd love them as much as she did.

And if her suspicions were correct, was marrying him the route she wanted to take? The route she *should* take?

She sighed. Perhaps she hadn't given him the personal attention he'd been used to receiving before their engagement, but the children had required everything she'd had and then some. Maybe being separated for several weeks would help her—and Dwight—see the situation more clearly. Wasn't there an adage about absence making the heart grow fonder? She hoped so.

Forcing her personal life out of her mind, Megan read the notes she'd written. She had nothing to add, so she scrawled her signature, clicked her pen and closed the chart.

By the time she'd stuck it in the slot for the medical records staff, Gene returned, carrying two paper sacks in one hand. He gave her the smaller of the two.

'Here are your goodies,' he proclaimed.

'Thanks.' She felt the bag. 'Still warm.'

'Fresh out of the oven, or so I'm told.'

She rose. 'Then I'll have mine with coffee. If you need me, you know where I'll be.'

'OK, but don't forget. If you see Dr Taylor...'

'I'll tell him you're looking for him,' she promised.

'You have to tell her,' Jonas Taylor matter-of-factly advised his colleague, Dwight Fleming, while they hovered near the coffee-maker in the ER staff lounge.

Dwight heaved a sigh. 'Yeah. The question is, when? Before I leave or after I get back?'

'If I knew my decision was final, I wouldn't want this hanging over my head for several more weeks,' Jonas answered firmly. 'It's not fair to Megan.'

'Waiting will only prolong the inevitable, I suppose.'

'Exactly.' Being the newest kid on Stanton Community Hospital's block, Jonas was surprised Dwight had cornered him to discuss such a personal matter. He hardly knew the man. Giving Dwight a plastic surgery referral and joining him for a beer with a group of hospital personnel who'd gone to the First Base sports bar after a harrowing night in the ER made him a passing acquaintance, not a father confessor.

'On the other hand,' Jonas continued, 'maybe you should talk to someone else. Someone who—'

'I can't.'

'Why not?'

Dwight ran one hand over his face. 'Because everyone who knows Megan sympathizes with her. All I hear is how wonderful she is to be raising her brother's two kids. A regular saint, if you get my drift.'

'And you'll look like the bad guy,' Jonas guessed.

Dwight nodded miserably. 'The thing is, I think she's wonderful, too. She's one of a kind.'

Jonas privately agreed. Megan Erickson was one of the best ER nurses he'd worked with and he'd been around enough of them to know. She was bright, beautiful and possessed a calm personality that came in handy during moments of tension. The unit functioned like a well-oiled machine when she was on duty and limped along when she wasn't.

She'd earned the respect of everyone and received more than her fair share of admiring male glances, Jonas's included. How could he not? Everything about her breathed vitality, from the shimmery highlights in her short chestnut brown hair to the confident way she carried herself.

Her hazel eyes shone with intelligence and humor and the ready smile on her face was always a welcome sight. The entire package of a pert nose, creamy skin and a body that filled out her scrub suits in all the right places could turn a man completely inside out.

He would have liked to have asked her out, but two things held him back—the diamond on her finger and the fact that she was the type who *should* wear a ring on her finger. She was the kind of woman a fellow took home to meet his family, the kind he steered clear of with every ounce of his being.

It didn't stop him from dreaming, though.

Regardless of her marital status, she was a bright spot in a department that needed one more often than not. Her upbeat attitude was surprising really, when the rumors said that her life for the past few years hadn't been a bed of roses.

And he was recommending that her boyfriend, no, *fiancé*, add another thorn to her collection.

Some days, life was a royal pain.

'Anyway,' Dwight continued, 'you're a man who's been around. I figure you could give me an unbiased opinion. See things from my side of the fence.'

Normally, Jonas kept his nose out of other people's problems. It seemed a waste of energy to get caught up in coworkers' personal lives when, other than his years in medical school and residency, the longest he'd stayed in any one place had been eighteen months. But Dwight *had* asked for his advice and as much as he hated to get involved, as much as he knew this would hurt Megan in the short term, he had to be truthful. Honesty was the best policy.

As for seeing things from Dwight's side of the fence, he saw them quite plainly. While others might encourage Dwight to stick with Megan for the sake of the kids, Jonas couldn't for that very reason. No marriage was better than a bad one and he respected her too much to steer her in the wrong direction.

'Like I said, it won't get easier the longer you wait,' he cautioned with his voice of experience. He might be only a year or two older than Dwight, but he'd packed a lot of living in his thirty-four years and knew what he was talking about.

'You're right. I've been stewing over this since last summer, when her brother was killed.'

'It's April, man!' Jonas was incredulous. If Dwight had harbored doubts for that length of time, he didn't have any business tying the knot. 'Are you serious?'

Dwight shrugged and his face turned ruddy. 'I thought my feelings would change, but they haven't. Then, a few weeks ago, she began dropping hints that we should get our wedding plans back on track.'

'If you're waiting for Megan's family responsibilities to fade,' Jonas mused aloud, 'you're out of luck. They won't disappear in the next six months or the next six years. You're either in for the duration or you're not. It's better to come clean now rather than later.' He rinsed out his coffee-mug and refilled it with the strong brew that was the mainstay of the ER.

'I don't know how to tell her. What shall I say?'

'Be honest. You owe it to her.' Megan would probably

be upset—any woman would be when her intended cried off—but she was a logical person. For all he knew, she might have even sensed their break-up was imminent. He certainly would if *his* fiancée had dragged her feet for a year over setting a date.

Not that he had a fiancée, or even *wanted* one, of course. The M-word wasn't part of his vocabulary.

Jonas drank his coffee, conscious of how Dwight's gaze had become speculative. 'Now what?' he asked.

'Have you done this before?' Dwight asked.

'Done what? Broken off an engagement?' At Dwight's nod, Jonas grinned. 'I've walked away from a number of interesting women, but nothing was serious. How can a man settle for one when there are so many to choose from?'

He fell back on his usual excuse for his single state. It was easier and simpler to confirm the conclusion people had drawn than to explain the real reason. In fact, he wasn't sure what his real reason was, other than he knew he wasn't cut out for commitment. He had nothing against marriage— the finest people he knew were married—but that particular state wasn't for him.

And although Dwight Fleming reeked of respectability and seemed to be a family man, he obviously wasn't interested in matrimony either. At least, not to a woman saddled with two kids and an ailing parent.

If a man truly loved a woman, he wouldn't let those details stop him, which only went to show that Dwight didn't love her. Yup, he was definitely doing Megan a favor.

'Just tell her the truth,' Jonas repeated. 'That you're not ready. That you want to pursue your career before you settle down with a mortgage payment, a mini-van and a St Bernard.'

Dwight squared his shoulders. 'OK. I will.'

'When?' At the moment, Dwight seemed ready, willing and able, but if he didn't act while his courage was up, he'd probably postpone it until tomorrow. Worse yet, he'd do as he'd threatened and wait until he returned from his month-long medical missions trip.

Megan didn't deserve to be left in limbo by any man, much less one as shallow as Dwight.

'I'll catch her before her shift ends.'

Jonas might not be the world's most romantic fellow, but he could think of a more appropriate backdrop for this conversation than the ER. 'Wouldn't you rather go somewhere more…ah, private?'

Dwight shook his head. 'I can't take her to dinner because she won't be able to find a sitter at such short notice. Trying to have a heart-to-heart at her place is impossible because of all the interruptions. The kids are in the hospital day care, and they won't mind if she's late. No, this is the best place.'

Jonas disagreed. 'At least take her to the restaurant across the street. It won't be busy at three-thirty.'

'Oh.' Dwight blinked as he considered the suggestion. 'That might work.'

Jonas clapped him on his shoulder. 'You can do this. And nothing says that you can't be friends when this is all over.' Whenever Jonas's relationships drew to a close, he always remained on amiable terms with the women involved. He attributed his success to faithfully following a few simple rules. One, he never made plans further ahead than the upcoming weekend. Two, he steered away from deeply personal topics of conversation and, three, he never, *ever* met their families.

'I suppose so.' Dwight didn't seem convinced, which was understandable because he didn't follow Jonas's foolproof rules. Maybe when this was all over, he'd let him in on his hard-learned secret.

'And you'll tell her everything.'

'I'll tell her everything.'

\* \* \*

Eagerly anticipating her first bite, Megan headed for the lounge at the far end of the department, next to the supply storage area. It was large enough to hold a twelve-person conference table and doubled as the formal meeting place for department gatherings. At other times, it was simply a place where staff could take a few minutes to fortify themselves between patients.

Because no one usually had time to linger, she was pleasantly surprised to find Dwight and Jonas standing near the coffee-pot, but they were too engrossed in their conversation to notice her arrival. Hating to interrupt, she quietly retrieved her personal cup from the cupboard and waited for them to finish their discussion.

'And you'll tell her everything?' Jonas asked.

'I'll tell her everything,' Dwight promised. 'Right after—Megan. I didn't see you come in.'

She ambled toward the pot and gave herself a half-serving, curious about the guilty flush on his face. 'Obviously not. By the way, Jonas, Gene has the lab results you were waiting for.'

He drained his mug with one gulp. 'Thanks.'

'You guys look rather intense for the morning being so dull,' Megan commented. 'What's up?'

Jonas's face underwent a transformation as he flashed one of his killer smiles at her. 'Intense? Not us.'

She dismissed him with one wave of her free hand and sent an enquiring glance at Dwight. 'I heard what he said. "You'll tell her everything." You two were talking about that girl who was in yesterday's car crash, weren't you?'

An eighteen-year-old had been rear-ended and, because she hadn't worn her seat belt, she'd flown head first through the windshield. The damage to her face had been extensive and Jonas had called in the best plastic surgeon available—Dwight.

The men exchanged a private glance that she couldn't read. 'Yeah, we were,' Jonas began.

'No,' Dwight said.

Megan raised one eyebrow. 'This wasn't a trick question, guys.'

Dwight's shoulders seemed to straighten before her eyes. 'No, we weren't discussing that patient. We weren't talking shop at all.'

The lack of his normally jovial demeanor was like a warning flag to her intuition. Her light-hearted mood dimmed. 'Oh. Then who—?' she began.

'We have to talk,' Dwight said, his voice strong and sure.

Jonas wondered how he'd extricate himself from this situation. Where was a code blue when he needed one? The combination of worry and hope on Megan's face mirrored the look he saw so often on family members's faces before he broke the oftentimes bad news about their loved one's condition. Knowing he'd played a role in the upcoming drama, he didn't want to stick around to watch.

'I'd better look into those lab results,' he muttered, certain that neither party heard him. Their gazes were too focused on each other to notice if he stayed or left, and this was definitely a time when three was a crowd.

He slipped out of the room, careful to close the door with a quiet snick. He should have felt good that Dwight had found his gumption, but he didn't. With Megan's expression haunting him, how could he?

'I thought I could marry you,' Dwight said flatly, 'but I can't.'

Megan stood stock still, feeling as if the bottom had dropped out of her world once again. 'You can't handle marriage with me or the fact that I'm now a package deal.'

He winced. 'You know I love you, Meggie.'

She scoffed at his pet name, a name that she didn't ever want to hear again. 'If you did, we wouldn't be having this conversation.'

'The truth is, I'm not ready to be an instant father. I talked it over with Jonas, and although I want children, I don't want them now and certainly don't want a houseful.'

'Two don't make a houseful,' she carefully pointed out, wondering what had precipitated his sudden case of cold feet. Then again, if his doubts had surfaced when hers had, this had been coming for quite some time.

'If you felt this way, why didn't you say something before now?' Being a private person, she hated the idea of Dwight taking a relative stranger into his confidence, especially one who practically had staff falling at his feet in their rush to provide whatever he requested.

'We could have worked something out,' she continued.

'When and how?' he demanded. 'I've hardly had a minute alone with you for the last year. Whenever I mentioned the subject, you dismissed my suggestions outright.'

'Suggestions?' Her voice rose. 'You knew from the beginning that I couldn't place Angela and Trevor into foster-care any more than I could encourage my mother to put my dad in a nursing home. That day will come soon enough, thank you very much. But if you wanted advice, why did you choose Jonas? Since when is *he* the expert on relationships?'

'I wanted a fresh, unbiased opinion. He only confirmed what I already thought.'

'You chose him because he'd tell you what you wanted to hear. Given his lifestyle, he wouldn't advise you to stick it out and work through these issues.' She hated hearing the tremble in her voice and swallowed hard.

'This wasn't a spur-of-the-moment choice, Meggie.' At her frown, he corrected himself. 'Megan. I've thought about this for a long time. I just didn't have the nerve to say anything. Since I'm leaving in ten days, I thought it would be best to wrap up my unfinished business before I go.'

Once she'd been the light of his life, or so he'd told her. Now she was merely unfinished business.

Unwilling to give him the satisfaction of knowing how much his rejection hurt, she twisted the solitaire from her finger and forced herself to sound as unaffected as if he were cancelling a movie date instead of their future. 'Consider it wrapped up, Dwight.' She placed the ring on the counter rather than in his hand. 'All nice and neat in one tidy little throw-away package.'

Abandoning her mug and cookies when she really wanted to toss them at Dwight's head, she started for the door.

'I'm sorry, Megan, but it's for the best,' he called out after her.

She didn't intend to argue. Her emotions had lumped together in her throat and made it difficult to speak without sounding as if she were begging. If he could destroy her dreams with the same clinical detachment he showed his patients, then her pride wouldn't let her show any reaction either.

Pausing, she cast a backward glance at him. 'It probably is,' she agreed with a calm she didn't feel. Then, before anything more could be said, she left the room.

Overloaded by the array of emotions that had struck within minutes, her thoughts froze as she wandered down the hall without a destination in mind. She felt utterly and completely numb until she saw Jonas sitting behind the nurses' station where he'd claimed her usual spot. The pity in his eyes as he met her gaze brought embarrassed heat to her face.

Immediately she changed direction and strode toward the nearest exam room. The urge to say something she might later regret was too strong for her to ignore. Counting syringes and tongue depressors would keep her busy with mindless activity—something she desperately needed at the moment.

She didn't get far before Jonas appeared at her side. 'Are you OK?' he asked.

'What do you think?' she snapped as she blinked to hold back the tears forming in her eyes.

'Look. I'm sorry—'

'I don't want to discuss it.'

He continued as if she hadn't interrupted. 'We have two patients arriving in a couple of minutes. An industrial accident. If you can't manage, I'll talk to your supervisor—'

'I know my job, Dr Taylor,' she retorted, 'and I certainly don't need any more of your *assistance*.'

He fell silent as her intended barb struck home.

Hoping to leave him behind, she started to walk away, but he stopped her with a firm grip on her elbow. 'If you can't function at peak efficiency—'

'I can function just fine,' she snapped.

'Hold out your hands,' he commanded.

'What?'

He let go of her arm. 'Hold out your hands,' he repeated.

'For the love of...' She bit off the rest of her comment. Jonas wouldn't stop pestering her until she complied, and she wasn't in the mood to be hounded. She held out both hands, palms facing downward.

'Now what?' she demanded.

'Steady as a rock, eh?' He raised one eyebrow.

She looked down and the sight was totally unexpected. Both hands trembled as if she were afflicted with her father's Parkinson's disease.

Immediately she crossed her arms to hide the visible sign of her emotional distress and stiffened her spine. 'I'll be fine.'

Jonas studied her for a second but before he could comment the automatic ambulance bay doors whooshed open. Megan's personal life disappeared into the background as her training took over and she met the two paramedics who wheeled in a burly patient. He was in full cervical spine immobilization and she ran through her mental checklist of procedures to follow.

Sam, the familiar forty-five-year-old paramedic, delivered the report. 'BP is 140 over 80, pulse is 102, respirations sixteen. Patient is fifty-two and was alert when we arrived. He complained of his neck and chest hurting, along with his right hand, leg and ankle. His name is Eldon Lawver.'

Megan noticed the splints on the affected extremities. 'Trauma two,' she directed.

'What happened?' Jonas asked as they wheeled Lawver's gurney into the trauma room and were immediately joined by two more nurses.

'According to witnesses, one of Lawver's coworkers ran amok with a forklift. Instead of hitting the brake, he hit the accelerator and ran into a row of fifty-five-gallon drums. When they rolled, they knocked this guy over and pinned him against a wall.'

'And the driver?'

'He's coming in the next ambulance.'

Megan started hooking Lawver up to the array of monitoring equipment standing by, while Jonas began his own physical assessment. 'I want a complete set of films, starting with the C-spine,' he ordered. 'And get the usual CBC, blood chemistries and urinalysis.'

Megan knew the prime concern at the moment was the patient's airway. Any injuries in the cervical vertebrae 3, 4 and 5 would cause a loss of control of the diaphragm. It was a good sign that their patient didn't seem to be having any respiratory difficulty.

To save precious moments, she prepared to draw the blood sample herself rather than wait for the lab technician to arrive. Although the procedure went quickly and without incident, she was frustrated to notice the slight tremor in her hands was still there.

It certainly didn't help matters when she looked up after she'd finished and saw Jonas's unreadable intent gaze resting upon her.

Fortunately, the X-ray tech appeared with the portable unit and she scrambled to get out of her way. A few minutes later the commotion outside heralded the second ambulance's arrival and Megan's assignment as triage nurse for the day gave her an opportunity to escape Jonas's watchful eye. At least for a short while.

'I'll be there before long,' Jonas called out after her.

Nodding her acknowledgment, she hurried out of Lawyer's room to send the latest arrival to trauma three.

'I'm fine and I wanna go back to work,' the young man on the gurney yelled to anyone who would listen.

'You'll go back when the doc says you can go back,' the EMT told him.

'What's your name?' Megan asked her patient.

'Carl. Carl Walker.'

'Well, Carl,' she said in her no-nonsense voice, 'I see you have a knot on your head. Do you feel pain any place else?'

Andy, one of the EMTs snickered. 'He's not feeling *any* pain, if you know what I mean.'

'I'm fine and I jus' wanna leave.' The fellow slurred his words and as Megan leaned across him to place the pulse oximeter on his finger she caught a whiff of his breath. The fumes were strong enough to make her eyes cross.

An on-the-job accident involving alcohol presented a host of legal issues. She'd have to make sure their documentation was absolutely perfect because this case would most likely wind up in court. In the meantime, Carl needed assessment.

'Do you hurt anywhere?' she asked him again.

'I just wanna go home,' he crooned.

'At least he's a happy drunk,' Andy remarked.

'Did you find anything other than the bump on his head?'

He shook his head. 'Not a thing. We'd expected more injuries after falling off a forklift, but I guess he was too limp to hurt himself. He'll probably walk away with a few muscle aches, a couple of bruises and a helluva hangover.'

Megan hoped that Mr Lawver would be as fortunate.

'OK,' she said. 'Thanks, guys.' She turned to Gene. 'Keep an eye on him while I see what Dr Taylor wants us to do. If he starts throwing up, be sure he doesn't choke.'

Gene glanced at Carl with an expression akin to disgust. 'If you say so.'

Suddenly, Megan realized what she'd done. She'd asked a man who'd lost his brother to a drunk driver six months ago to take care of an inebriated patient. Memories and unresolved issues would make this case more difficult than the usual DUI case.

'I'm sorry, Gene. I'll send someone to take over for you.'

He shrugged as if the situation didn't bother him, but his set jaw suggested otherwise. 'A DUI was bound to wander into the ER, but I can handle this. I *will* handle this.'

She hesitated. 'Are you sure?'

'Yes.' The grin he gave her seemed forced. 'Just don't evaluate me on my compassion and bedside manner.'

Megan smiled. 'I won't. I'll be back a.s.a.p.' Just thinking of Jonas brought back the tension she'd felt earlier. Working together would be tough, at least for awhile, and she wondered if a vacation would help her get over her anger at him for not minding his own business.

Probably not, she decided. She didn't have enough vacation hours for that to occur.

She returned to trauma two, surprised to see the block and collar on Lawver's neck was gone. Her interest in the patient once again helped her relegate her personal issues with Jonas to the background. 'How is he?' she asked.

'His spinal column is OK, but he has a fractured clavicle, a dislocated shoulder, a sprained wrist, a fractured tibia and ankle.'

'Wow.'

'No kidding, but he's still a lucky man, all things considered.'

'Internal bleeding?'

'None that we can see so far, but he hasn't gone for his CT scan yet. He'll be here for a while, I'm sure. I don't know what the orthopedic fellows will want to fix first.' He motioned in the direction of the other room. 'How's our other victim?'

'Other than his breath is eighty-proof, he's stable.'

'Drunk?'

'I'd say so, but you'll need to order a blood-alcohol level.'

'OK. While you're drawing his blood sample, get enough for the usual CBC and chemistry panel. I'll be there in a few minutes.'

'Will do.'

Megan returned to Walker's room in time to hear his latest unrecognizable melody. 'How is he?' she asked Gene as she gathered her blood tubes and supplies to collect a sample of Carl's blood.

'Other than he can't carry a tune with both hands, he's docile enough,' the EMT replied as he recorded the latest blood-pressure reading.

'Let's hope he stays that way.' She leaned over Carl to draw his attention while she tried not to inhale. 'Carl? I need to take a blood sample.'

'I don't feel so good,' he moaned.

'Hold on,' Gene told him before he went to the cupboards across the room to look for an emesis basin.

Megan tugged on a fresh pair of latex gloves before she pushed up his short sleeve and tied on the tourniquet. After swabbing the skin with an alcohol-free disinfectant, she positioned her needle, bevel up, and was pleased to see her steady hand. Too bad Jonas wasn't around to see this, she thought as she inserted the needle into Carl's vein.

Immediately, belligerence replaced Carl's former easy-going nature. He rose up, howling as he flailed his arms to get away from this latest insult. 'What are you doing?' he yelled.

Naturally, Megan couldn't hold his arm still and the needle slid out of his arm. 'Don't move,' she commanded, feeling as if she were wrestling an octopus with one hand. Blood ran down his arm and he fought her attempt to release the tourniquet and staunch the flow.

'No,' he cried. 'Don't want to.'

Gene entered the fray, but before he was able to subdue him, Carl shook off Megan's grip with a near-superhuman strength.

Something seemed to bite her palm, and she looked on in horror as she saw the used needle buried to the hilt in the fleshy part of her thumb, an inch or so above her wrist.

Jonas, who'd appeared as if by magic to help Gene, muttered an expletive that she mentally echoed.

'Damn it, Megan.' He sounded aggrieved. 'What have you done to yourself?'

# CHAPTER TWO

'I KNEW I should have let someone cover for you,' Jonas continued vehemently.

'I didn't stick myself on purpose,' Megan snapped as she dropped the offending needle into a sharps collector. Did he think she wasn't strong enough to weather Dwight's rejection without falling to pieces? How inept did he think she was?

'For your information, I was *not* careless. Ask Gene.'

'She wasn't,' Gene confirmed. 'If anything, I shouldn't have been across the room at the time.'

'We can hold our post-mortem later, when there aren't patients needing us.' Megan stripped off her gloves to inspect the wound more closely. The site was still bleeding, and she let the flow continue as she headed toward the sink and turned on the taps. Hopefully, any of the potential viruses in Carl's blood would wash out with her own.

'Scrub your hands with soap. Use the germicidal stuff,' Jonas instructed as he joined her.

'I will.' She stared at her bleeding palm, noticing how her tremor had returned, and with good reason. Needlestick injuries weren't to be treated lightly. Health-care workers had contracted life-threatening diseases over such innocent incidents, and the possibility of her joining those ranks sent a fresh wave of dread through her. Being jilted just a short time ago suddenly seemed so minor when she considered what *could* happen in the upcoming weeks and months.

'Call what's-her-name,' he ordered. 'The infection control nurse.'

'Susan Forbes,' she supplied, surprised that Jonas had

forgotten. From what she'd seen so far, he recalled people's names with an ease that was downright disgusting.

'Yeah, Susan.' He continued to hover when she wanted to be left alone to berate herself in peace and quiet.

'Did you need something? Or were you watching my technique?'

His grin was one of those enticing smiles that melted her female coworkers into a puddle. She'd felt the effects of it herself on occasion, although the diamond on her finger had kept her from succumbing to his charisma.

Now the empty space on her hand would remind her of his meddling and make her immune to his charm. She couldn't have chosen a better talisman than that.

'Do you really want me to answer?' he asked with a decided twinkle in his eye.

Megan glared at him. 'Forget I said anything. Don't you have a patient to examine?'

'He isn't going anywhere. I just wanted to tell you not to panic.'

He'd obviously seen the tremor in her hands as she'd rinsed the suds off her outstretched palm and had guessed at the particular merry-go-round her thoughts were riding. Yet admitting her weakness only seemed to make the risks more real.

She raised her chin defiantly. 'Who said I was panicking?'

He leaned close enough to speak in her ear. Close enough for her to faintly smell the decidedly male-scented soap he used. 'You can't fool me, Megan. I'd have to be blind not to see how pale and shaky you are and I know the scenarios that are swirling around in your head. You aren't the first person I've treated under these circumstances.'

She was surprised to realize how easily he read her, but

as much as she wanted to deny his observation, she couldn't.

'Hang onto the notion that not every exposure ends up badly,' he added kindly. 'Think positive.'

She inhaled a cleaning breath and nodded. He was right. Worrying prematurely was counterproductive, but it was easier said than done. 'I'll try.'

'Good girl. I'll check out our patient while you finish up and call Susan. Then we'll take care of you.' He patted her shoulder before he returned to Carl's side.

Megan was grateful that he hadn't waited for a response. The way he'd said *we'll take care of you* brought tears to her eyes and a lump to her throat. It had been so long since anyone had taken care of her, so long since anyone had worried about her. She'd been the strong one in the family, holding things together and encouraging her mother to hold onto hope when her father had been diagnosed with Parkinson's four years ago.

It had also been Megan who'd picked up the pieces after her brother's and sister-in-law's deaths. She didn't mind raising the two children they'd left behind, but after a year of being a single parent she'd looked forward to sharing those responsibilities with Dwight. Angela and Trevor needed a father's influence but, thanks to the man a few feet away from her, neither would receive it.

*Deal with one issue at a time*, she told herself as she towel-dried her hands. Right now she had more pressing worries than a broken engagement.

Jonas glanced at the clipboard listing Carl's medical data while Megan talked in the background on the telephone, presumably to Susan. So far, his patient had exhibited nothing out of the ordinary, other than he'd clearly exceeded the legal alcohol limit. The few bumps and bruises he found were only to be expected. Physically, Carl had come through his escapade unscathed, but he'd probably lose his job. With this on his employment record, he'd have a tough time finding anyone else to hire him.

That, however, wasn't Jonas's concern. Carl Walker's hepatitis and HIV status were.

'Accident,' Carl slurred as he momentarily surfaced from his drunken fog. 'Did you know I had an accident?'

'We know,' Jonas told him. 'That's why you're in the hospital.'

Carl squinted. 'You the doctor?'

'Yes.'

'Am I hurt bad? I don't feel like I'm hurt. Other than I have a headache.'

A hangover was more like it. 'You're fine,' Jonas told him. 'But we're going to need a blood sample.'

'Again? Don't like needles.'

His aversion was good news. If he meant what he was mumbling, then the likelihood of him shooting drugs was slim. It also suggested that the odds of him carrying HIV or one of the hepatitis viruses was low, and the chances of Megan developing problems were equally negligible.

'We tried, but you didn't co-operate,' Jonas told him, 'so this time you *will* lie still and not twitch so much as a muscle. When you fought the way you did, our nurse stuck herself with the same needle she used on you. Now we have to run extra tests for hepatitis and HIV.' He paused. 'Do you understand what I'm saying?'

'Yeah. Extra tests.'

'And we'll need a urine sample.' It was common practice to run drug screens on the parties involved in workplace accidents and Jonas also wanted the lab to check for kidney damage.

'OK. I could use the john.'

Jonas wasn't feeling particularly benevolent toward Carl at the moment and decided he could stand to suffer for a few minutes. 'First the blood sample.' He began the procedure and this time the only muscle Carl moved involved his mouth.

'I'm healthy as a horse,' he boasted.

'I'm glad to hear it,' Jonas answered, aware of Megan returning to handle her normal nursing duties.

'My girlfriend's not, though,' he mourned. 'Got her results yesterday. Bad news, they were.'

'Oh, really?' Jonas popped the final tube into the needle holder.

'It was positive. They say there's no cure.' Carl peered at Jonas through bloodshot eyes. 'You're a doctor. Is that true?'

'It depends. What are you talking about?'

'HIV. They haven't found a cure yet, have they?'

Jonas's gaze immediately traveled to Megan's face. Her complexion seemed to whiten another shade and her eyes appeared haunted.

'No,' he answered. 'They haven't.'

'That's what she said. I couldn't handle what was gonna happen, so I had a few drinks.'

Jonas suspected he'd had more than a few. In any case, if his girlfriend had tested positive for HIV, then Carl could easily be positive, too. Which meant... He didn't want to think about what it meant.

'Have you been screened, too?' he asked as he withdrew the needle and taped cotton over the spot.

'I was going to do that tomorrow.'

'Well, Carl, because of the circumstances, we're going to do it this afternoon. I'll have you sign the permission forms.'

'That's good. Can I go home now?'

'Not yet.' He handed the tubes to Gene. 'Take care of these.'

'Will do.'

'Dr Taylor?' The ER ward clerk appeared in the doorway. 'As soon as you're finished here, there are some men from Mulligan's Manufacturing who want to talk to you.'

'They're going to have to wait.' Jonas grabbed Megan's arm and ushered her past the clerk into a private patient cubicle. Her previously pale face now appeared as frozen as ice and she seemed far too calm for his liking. Shell-shocked, he decided.

'I know what you're thinking,' he said, 'but don't. When Susan gets here—'

'She's not coming.'

'What?'

'She's not on duty today.'

'OK, then here's what we're going to do,' he said, aware that she knew the proper procedures as well as he did but was probably too rattled to think clearly. 'I'll draw your blood sample and the lab will test you for hepatitis B and C, as well as HIV. Your results will be your baseline while Carl's will show us if he carries any infectious viruses. If he's negative, then we're home free.'

'And if he's not?'

'If he does carry those viruses, then we'll test you in six weeks to determine if you *become* positive to those same viruses. But before we start thinking that far ahead, let's get these initial results. Don't jump to conclusions.'

'With his girlfriend HIV positive, don't you think there's a good chance that he will be, too?'

'Not necessarily. There are a lot of variables coming into play. For all we know, they've just started dating.'

'Then again, they might have been seeing each other for years.'

'The statistics show that the average risk for contracting the virus in these types of injuries is point three per cent. If his test is positive, we'll start you on a regimen of antiretrovirals. We only have to wait an hour and then you can stop worrying.'

She looked at him and her expression made him want to hug her. 'Or start.'

'Look. I checked him over thoroughly. He shows no signs of having an active infection. He's not jaundiced and none of his internal organs appear enlarged. He's probably right about being healthy,' he said as he assembled his equipment and tubes. 'My first question for you is, have you been vaccinated for hepatitis B?'

'With all three doses,' she said. 'And my antibody level was fine the last time we checked.'

'Then you won't need the hep. B immune globulin,' he mused aloud. 'There's nothing we can do about the possible exposure to hepatitis C, except wait and see.'

'No offense, but your advice ranks up there with, "Take two aspirin and call me in the morning."'

Jonas smiled as he tied the tourniquet around Megan's arm and deftly proceeded to fill the tubes, conscious of her lemony scent teasing his nose.

'Don't knock the first prescription we learned in med school,' he protested mildly. 'It's helped countless people since Bayer marketed it in 1899.'

'He discovered it that long ago?'

'Actually, a chemist by the name of Felix Hoffmann, who worked for the Bayer Company, synthesized it in 1897. It took two years of hospital trials before it was released.'

'Really?'

Pleased that she'd relaxed and her color had started to return, he continued his trivia recitation. 'Sure. They had their own bureaucracies to fight. Did you know they chose the name because "A" was for the "acetyl" part of its chemical name and "spirin" referred to *Spirea*, which was the genus name for the shrub that was a source of salicylic acid?'

'I'm impressed.'

He tapped his head with his free hand. 'I have all sorts of information stored away up here.' Then, because he wanted to keep her thoughts diverted, he asked, 'So what can a guy do in Stanton during his free time?'

'If you're asking about night life, you're asking the wrong person.'

'Surely there's a club or a restaurant you can recommend.'

'Ask your date. She'll have a preference, I'm sure.'

'Hey,' he protested, pretending affront. 'I do eat some meals by myself.'

'Don't you cook at home?'

'A little,' he admitted, unwilling to mention that he'd learned to prepare all types of food when he'd been an army brat, moving around the country with his dad. 'But cooking for one isn't always worth the effort.'

'I suppose not,' she said. 'Rick's Ribs is great if you like steak or barbecue. The Pagoda has excellent Oriental food and Connie's Creations serves great sandwiches and baked goods. Her desserts are out of this world.'

He finished his task and labeled her samples. 'Then she makes pies?' he asked, thinking of his favorite, lemon meringue.

Megan smiled and he was pleased to see her face had regained more of its healthy color. 'With a crust that melts in your mouth. They're rather expensive, but worth every penny.'

Jonas suspected that she didn't indulge herself very often. With a trim figure like hers, she either avoided sweets or burned off the calories running after her niece and nephew. If the key to a man's heart was through his stomach, he was willing to see if the adage applied to women as well. 'Where is this place?'

'On the south end of Lakewood. You can't miss it.'

'What do people around here do on the weekends?'

'Mow their yards. Clean house. Do laundry.'

'For fun,' he corrected.

She shrugged. 'We have two golf courses, one public and one private. There are a few tennis courts, a bowling alley and a swimming pool.'

'What about car-racing or skydiving?'

'There's a race track on the west end of town, but it's amateur, not professional. I've heard there's a skydiving club at the airport, but I don't know of anyone who belongs. Are those your hobbies?'

He shrugged. 'At one time, but I haven't done either for years. I've become staid in my old age and got hooked on golf. Do you play?'

'I used to.'

'Why did you stop?'

'An eighteen-month-old and a four-year-old aren't exactly welcome on the course,' she said wryly.

'So find a babysitter.'

'They're rather clingy right now and I hate to leave them with someone else unless absolutely necessary. When they're older and more independent, I'll play again.'

After inspecting her arm and taping cotton over the site, he straightened. 'All done.'

'I'm impressed. I barely felt the needle go in. You have a light touch.'

If she only knew what else he'd like to touch... As far as he was concerned, Dwight was a fool. Yet, as much as Jonas would have liked to have taken up where Dwight had left off, he couldn't. Inevitably he'd hurt her and he refused to do that, regardless of how much he'd like it to be otherwise.

'All part of the service,' he joked. 'Why don't you take five, drink a cup of coffee or take care of paperwork until we hear from the lab?'

'I'd rather stay busy.'

'I guessed you'd say that. Honestly, though. There isn't anything going on that we can't handle without you,' he pointed out.

'You still have to admit Mr Lawver and talk to the Mulligan Manufacturing people. Someone also has to call Carl's girlfriend so he can leave if his tests are negative. All the paperwork for my little incident is waiting, not to mention our other patients.'

'OK.' He held up both hands in surrender. 'If you don't want to take a break, I can't force you. Just be careful.'

'Agreed.'

'And no sharp objects.'

She opened her mouth to object, then nodded. 'For now.'

Jonas expected her to rush back to work, but she surprised him by hesitating in the doorway. 'Thanks for everything.' Her tone was gruff, as if she didn't want to thank him, but courtesy demanded otherwise.

'My pleasure,' he answered.

Megan returned to the nurses' station and kept busy with paperwork. The orthopedic surgeon, Patrick Graham, arrived to review Mr Lawver's X-rays and organize his surgery. Jonas spent a long time with the men's supervisor from the chemical manufacturing plant while she checked the computer every ten minutes for Carl's lab results to appear.

Finally the printer whirred and page after page printed out. The blood-alcohol level was 180, which exceeded the legal limit. The toxicology report was negative and very encouraging. If a person abused alcohol, he often abused other drugs as well.

Carl's girlfriend arrived a few minutes later. A petite

brunette who dressed conservatively, Rae seemed like a nice young woman who was clearly concerned about her boyfriend. As soon as she'd introduced herself, Jonas ushered her into Carl's room, presumably to discuss the situation. Megan would have liked to have listened in on their conversation but, not having been invited to join them, she focused her attention and skills on a middle-aged man with chest pain.

With all the activity going on, the hour still seemed to drag by. When the lab hadn't called after ninety minutes, Megan watched for Jonas's return from Radiology and nabbed him as soon as she saw him.

'Can't you phone and ask for the results?'

'I did. They said they were extremely busy and were having to repeat some of the tests. The person I spoke to promised to page me in five minutes.'

She heaved a sigh and drew a tremulous breath. 'OK. Five minutes.'

Five minutes stretched to fifteen. When Jonas finally disappeared into his office to answer his page, Megan forced herself to wait patiently at the desk. The chest-pain patient chose that moment to summon her for a drink of water and she had no choice but to help him. Thanks to glass enclosing the trauma cubicles instead of solid walls, she saw Jonas walk past the central nurses' station and into Carl's room. Pasting a smile on her face for this patient's and his wife's sakes, she asked, 'Are you comfortable?'

'Relatively,' he replied.

'We should have your lab results shortly,' she told him, feeling as Jonas had that his problem was due to a severe epigastric incident rather than anything cardiac.

She returned to her charting and before long Jonas was escorting Carl and his girlfriend to the exit doors. The smile on his face helped ease the knot of tension in her stomach, until she saw that it was his professional, didn't-meet-his-eyes-type of smile.

She rose as he approached her. 'Well?' she demanded.

'Come with me,' he said, grabbing her arm and ushering her into his office. As soon as he closed the door, he spoke.

'The hepatitis B test was negative, but we won't have the hepatitis C results until tomorrow afternoon.'

Megan exhaled a cleansing breath. So far, so good. 'OK. What about the HIV?'

He hesitated. 'That's a little more complicated.'

'More complicated? How?'

'The first time they ran the test, Carl's sample was weakly positive.'

She gasped and slumped in the chair across from his desk. A positive HIV. A mental picture of the AIDS patients who'd visited the ER formed and she clenched her hands. Would she end up like them? It was too horrific a prospect to consider. She had parents who needed her, two children who couldn't lose another care-giver.

Jonas crouched beside her and covered her cold hands with his. The warmth he exuded did nothing to dispel the chill that had pierced her down to her marrow.

'The lab tech repeated the procedure and the results were plus-minus. Rather than run it a third time, the staff is going to send the sample to their reference lab for a Western blot, which is a more definitive test. Like I explained to Carl and Rae, this was only a screen and false positives aren't uncommon.'

He continued without stopping. 'The good news is that Carl's girlfriend is asymptomatic. Apparently, an earlier partner of hers has tested positive and that's why she went to the health department. With Carl's results being questionable, if he has the virus or, more accurately, the retrovirus, he has it in very low numbers.'

'Isn't that like saying a woman is only a "little bit pregnant"?'

'Perhaps, but to be on the safe side, I'm going to recommend you start the post-exposure prophylaxis immediately.'

Megan raised her eyebrow. 'Refresh my memory, please. What will that involve?'

'We'll use a combination of two drugs that currently inhibit or inactivate the HIV virus. If Carl's Western blot is negative, we can stop the therapy. If it isn't, we'll want to run more tests on him, especially his CD4+ T-cell counts.

'As you know,' he continued, 'HIV destroys those particular CD4+ lymphocytes, so the numbers present indicate the degree of infection. The lower the number, the worse the prognosis. I'm guessing that even if Carl is positive, his T-lymphocyte count is still good.'

'I understand,' she said, glad that he'd given the simplified version. 'And if I choose not to take the medications?'

'You're stacking the odds against yourself and I don't think you'll want to do that.'

'No.' Although she knew the PEP caused a lot of side effects, namely nausea and diarrhea, she couldn't afford the risk of *not* proceeding.

As if he knew what she'd decided, he explained further. 'Once we get all the results, we can re-evaluate your treatment. The drugs are toxic so, if you end up taking them for the full four weeks, we'll run a blood count and check out your renal and liver function in two weeks. The lab can run your baseline studies with the sample they already have, so you won't need to get stuck again.'

'Now, there's a bright spot in my day,' she said, tongue in cheek.

He grinned. 'I'm doing the best I can.' His mood sobered. 'And, finally, we'll do follow-up HIV tests at six and twelve weeks, and again at six months.'

'I could quote the protocol backwards and forwards, but now that it pertains to me, I can't think straight.' She forced a chuckle and finger-combed the hair off her forehead. 'Silly me.'

'It's not silly. Your reaction is perfectly normal. With the circumstances what they are, I still believe your chances of contracting anything serious are very slim.'

Megan looked into his eyes. 'But you can't give me a guarantee, can you?'

Jonas's gaze remained steady, but she read the apology in those dark depths. 'No, I can't.'

## CHAPTER THREE

JONAS squeezed Megan's left hand. 'I wish I could.'

For a moment, she didn't answer, but drew strength from his presence and firm grip. 'When do I start?'

'I'll call the pharmacy and as soon as they deliver the meds, I want you to take them immediately. Understood?'

She met his gaze and nodded. He squeezed her hand a final time as if satisfied that she would carry out his orders without question, then straightened.

'If you show any side effects, I can prescribe whatever you need to keep those under control. As you know, we're assuming Carl is HIV positive, so you must avoid any possible secondary transmissions,' he added. 'That means no donating blood or plasma at the next Red Cross blood drive or any time during the next six months.'

'I won't.' She certainly didn't want to put anyone else through this nightmare.

'And practice safe sex. Better yet, abstain.'

She felt herself warm under his admonition. Having this discussion with a man who could turn any woman's thoughts in that direction was, quite frankly, unsettling. For a moment she thought of what Dwight would say, then realized it didn't matter. He wasn't a part of her life any more.

The pain of his rejection seared her heart and she hid it behind her temper. 'I'm surprised you're bothering to tell me that.'

He frowned, clearly puzzled. 'Excuse me? I wouldn't be counseling you properly if I didn't mention it.'

Megan held up her free hand to display her bare finger.

'You don't need to worry if I'll spread anything to anyone. I'm un-engaged, remember?'

He shifted his weight. 'Look, Megan. About that. I'm really—'

She held up both hands like a traffic cop. 'Sorry,' she finished for him. 'Yes, I know. The fact remains that if not for you, I wouldn't be facing this alone.'

'I'm sure Dwight would—'

'Dwight lost the privilege of knowing anything about my private life. Don't you dare say a word to him—I don't care how good your friendship with him is.'

'I won't, but Dwight and I hardly know each other.'

'Oh, really. Could have fooled me.'

'Let me explain,' he began.

'You gave Dwight advice that he took to heart, and now he's out of my life. You should be pleased that you saved a fellow male from the noose of matrimony. No doubt, you painted a great picture of life in the fast lane, without anything or anyone tying you down, and he loved it. What's to explain?'

'That's not how it happened. He asked for my opinion.'

'And you happily gave it, without considering how it would affect three other people.'

'Not true. I *was* thinking of you.'

'Sorry, but I'm not convinced. Be that as it may, I don't want to discuss it.'

He ran one hand over his short hair. 'Fine,' he ground out. 'But getting back to our original subject, there are other people besides Dwight who can give you moral support.'

She scoffed. 'My parents have already lost a son. I can't drop this bombshell on them, nor would I want to.'

'I can understand that, but I was referring to myself.'

'You?' She couldn't believe him.

'Why not? I have broad shoulders.'

Without a conscious effort on her part, Megan's gaze

traveled over his torso. He was right. Not only were his shoulders wide, but they looked rock-solid. The idea of leaning on him was tempting, but she couldn't afford to use him as a crutch. However well meant his offer, Jonas's support would never be anything more than temporary and she needed something more permanent to hang onto.

And although she was being petty and illogical, he was still too closely linked with Dwight in her mind. She couldn't possibly be more than a professional acquaintance.

She rose with as much dignity as she could summon. 'Thanks, but I'll manage. Now, if you don't have anything to add, I'd better get back to work.'

He hesitated, almost as if he wanted to say something else, then didn't. 'OK.'

Megan threw herself into her duties. She told herself repeatedly, whenever her thoughts strayed onto the 'what-if' topic, that worry wouldn't help. She had to rest in the knowledge that she was doing everything medically possible to prevent an unfavorable outcome, otherwise she'd drive herself to drink, as Carl obviously had.

Her bigger concern at the moment was how she would tell her parents about her broken engagement. If she shared Dwight's reasons, it would make her mother feel guilty over not being able to care for Angela and Trevor. She had enough problems on her plate without Megan adding one more.

The youngsters would be the easiest to tell, she decided as she exchanged her scrub suit for a pair of jeans and a long-sleeved yellow knit turtleneck at the end of her shift. Neither one would look at her with pity or ask the penetrating questions that others would. Also, neither had grown close to Dwight, and under the circumstances it was probably a good thing. They wouldn't be traumatized when he disappeared out of their lives.

She slammed her locker door shut and hurriedly marked

her daily appointment book with the schedule Jonas had given her. At two and four weeks from today, a blood test to determine how her body was handling the toxic drugs. She counted out six weeks from today and found herself unable to write down HIV, so she put a huge X in the box instead. She repeated the process for twelve weeks, noticing that the six-month mark would be in October.

After updating her calendar to her satisfaction, she grabbed her purse and hurried to the exit. Working late had saved her from the usual locker-room small-talk and the inevitable rehash of the day's events. The hospital grapevine would spread the news about her broken engagement soon enough.

Her path to the department exit led past the nurses' station and fortunately only the afternoon shift ward clerk was there. As soon as Karen saw her, she waved at her and extended the phone. 'I'm glad I caught you,' she said. 'It's your mom.'

Megan placed her daily appointment book on the counter and grabbed the receiver.

'Hi, honey,' her mother, Nancy, said cheerfully. 'I'm glad I caught you. I wanted to tell you that your dad and I have decided to go to the park concert tonight since it's been such a beautiful day. Why don't you, Dwight and the kids come along? We can go out for ice cream afterwards.'

Megan pinched the bridge of her nose. 'I'm not sure about tonight,' she prevaricated. 'I've got a lot of things to do around the house.' Packing the odds and ends Dwight had left over the past year would keep her busy for several hours. Part of her was tempted to toss everything, including his hand-carved chess set, in the trash, but being vindictive would only show him how much he'd hurt her.

She had her pride.

'All right, dear, but if you should change your mind, call me before seven.'

'I will, Mom. Thanks for the invitation.'

She replaced the receiver, fighting an overwhelming sense of loss. Things would work out, she told herself. Her future might turn out far differently than she'd dreamed or even planned, but her life was bound to get better.

Just as soon as it stopped getting worse.

At six-thirty, after he'd turned over his duties to his replacement, Jonas stopped at the counter surrounding the nurses' desk and picked up a fat, pocket-sized appointment book. 'What's this?'

Karen looked up from the stack of papers in front of her. 'Megan left that. I thought she'd be back to pick it up by now. I'm guessing she doesn't realize it's here.'

'Probably not.' Considering the stress Megan had undergone today, forgetting her private appointment book wasn't surprising. 'I'm leaving myself,' he admitted. 'I can take it to her.'

'If she's as lost without hers as I am without mine, I'm sure she'd appreciate it if you did.'

Jonas wasn't as certain. Megan had rejected his overture of friendship but, then, who could blame her? Dwight would probably have summoned the nerve to have his heart-to-heart talk without Jonas advising him to do so, but Jonas's urging had changed the timetable. If Megan hadn't been so distraught over that, she might have been more alert when she was with Carl Walker. Oh, she'd deny any relationship between the two, but he was convinced the two incidents were related.

The stunned look on her face after she'd left the lounge had twisted the knife of guilt that had stabbed his chest. Then, when he'd seen the needle sticking in her palm, his protective instincts had grown by leaps and bounds and without any conscious effort on his part. After living his life by keeping everyone at a friendly distance, this new development was disturbing. For a man who didn't want any responsibility other than what came with his profession, he'd certainly contracted a huge case of it where Megan was concerned.

Lord knew, she'd tied him in knots this afternoon. Normally, he didn't care what people thought of him, but it seemed imperative that he explain how he'd only been looking out for everyone's best interests. Time would gradually show her that his advice had been appropriate for their situation, but his days in Stanton were limited and whether or not she realized it while he was still here was anyone's guess. He certainly didn't want to spend the next three months tiptoeing through a minefield in the ER. The department had enough tension without the staff adding more.

And now he'd been granted a golden opportunity to stitch the rip in their working relationship.

'Where does she live?' he asked.

'Over on MacArthur.' Patty dug out the phone book and looked up the listing. 'Fourteen hundred. That'll be easy to find. It's north of the elementary school, between Patton and Marshall.'

'Someone must have been a fan of military generals when they named the streets. I suppose Eisenhower is part of the same subdivision.'

Patty chuckled. 'Actually, he's in the row of presidential streets. Don't worry, it won't take long until you can find your way around like a native.'

Having lived in more cities around the world than he could count, Jonas had already started to learn the town's layout. He could find his way to the nearest grocery store, the movie theatre and the row of fast-food restaurants common to all of them. This weekend he'd check out the local golf courses. Residential addresses would come later, and he usually only paid attention to those where his current date lived.

For now, as long as he remembered the way to his place, he was fine. A mere two blocks from the hospital, the two-bedroom house that he temporarily called home stood in a quiet, elderly residential area and now, with this latest spell of warm weather, he walked home.

A dog slunk between his property and neighbors', only to stop in its tracks to gaze soulfully at him. Its dingy yellow coat was in need of a bath and a brushing, and its ribs were painfully evident. In spite of all that, Jonas could tell this had once been a beautiful golden retriever.

He'd always wanted a dog, but an animal had never fit into his family's lifestyle of moving from military base to military base. He'd toyed with the idea of getting a pet when he'd been in med school, but his schedule simply hadn't permitted it. He'd hardly had a minute to call his own during his internship and residency and several of his colleagues who'd been in the same boat had accepted the inevitable and given theirs away.

His life now wasn't much more conducive to taking on the added responsibility. Twelve-hour shifts five days a week meant that a dog would be on its own for most of its waking moments, which was a rotten way to treat man's best friend. Moving around the country like he did, he never knew if he'd have living quarters that could accommodate more than a goldfish, so he'd never given pet ownership a second thought.

This animal, with its large, pleading eyes and half-starved appearance only emphasized what he already knew. Pets were a responsibility and if its owner couldn't or wouldn't shoulder that responsibility, he or she didn't deserve them.

On the other hand, perhaps this one had simply become lost and needed help to find its way home.

'Hi, girl,' he said to the animal, but it stood there, looking wary and pitiful at the same time.

Jonas unlocked the front door and cast a final glance at it before he went inside. The retriever stood unmoving, as if waiting for Jonas to either chase it away or give it the food and water it desperately needed.

Certain it would leave once he was out of sight, Jonas closed the door and watched the retriever through the window. To his surprise, the creature simply sank onto the concrete driveway. With its head resting on its front paws, the dog appeared too weak to continue its search for someone who would care about its sorry state.

Knowing that he couldn't ignore the animal's misery and feel true to his Hippocratic oath, he filled a bowl with water. Taking the container and the leftover macaroni casserole he'd intended to eat for dinner outside, he set his offerings on the driveway in a shady spot near the bottom porch step.

'Here, girl,' he coaxed.

The retriever raised its head and stared at Jonas as if trying to determine if this was a trick. 'Come on,' he encouraged again. 'It's nothing fancy, but it's filling.'

The dog staggered to its feet and tentatively made its way toward the food.

'Go on. Eat. I won't hurt you.'

The animal hesitated, clearly weighing the risk of being mistreated versus missing another meal. As if he sensed Jonas's sincerity, the dog gave him one last cautious glance before it devoured the food and drank nearly all of the water. By the time it had licked the bowls clean and dry, its tail had started to wag.

As far as Jonas could tell, the retriever didn't have a collar. So much for trying to locate its owner.

'That's all I have,' he told the animal after it had backed away to watch his next move. 'Unless you want ice cream, and I don't think it's good for you.'

The retriever didn't seem concerned over his lack of dessert. Instead, it lay next to the house, in the shade under the eaves.

'This isn't your home,' he told the dog, but the animal made no attempt to move. After seeing how thirsty the poor thing had been, Jonas refilled the water bowl from the outside spigot.

'You're on your own, girl,' he told the animal before he went inside to change into jeans and his lucky golf T-shirt. When he returned to slide behind the wheel of his sporty blue convertible, he found the dog in the same place as he'd left it.

Hoping the retriever would move on once it realized that no one was home, he drove away. His stomach rumbled and he realized that he was going to interrupt what could be Megan's dinner hour. If he'd planned this, he could have taken her to try out one of those restaurants she'd recommended, but he hadn't. With two kids in tow, that wouldn't have been a good spur-of-the-moment idea. Maybe next time, he thought as he detoured to the street known as Fast-Food Row. Maybe next time.

'Did you lose your ring, Mommy?' Angela asked Megan as she fed Trevor his dinner. Although he preferred to hold the spoon himself, tonight he was tired and let Megan do the work.

'No, I didn't,' she answered, still unused to being called 'Mommy'. When the pair had first moved in with her, she had been 'Aunt Megan' and then Angie had decided that since Megan was now acting as her mother, she was 'Mommy Megan' as opposed to her 'real' mommy. Two weeks ago, she'd dropped Megan's name and now simply called her 'Mommy'.

'I gave it back to Dwight,' she added.

'How come?'

'Because we decided not to get married.' Megan spoke

nonchalantly, as if it had been as simple as choosing not to go to the park.

'Oh. Does that mean he won't be our daddy?'

Megan studied her niece's reaction, wondering how Dwight could possibly be fearful of raising these two sweet children. She leaned across the table and ran her hand over Angie's soft reddish-gold curls. 'Yes, sweetie, it does.'

Angie drew her eyebrows together. 'How come? Doesn't he like us?'

Out of the mouths of babes… 'It's not that he doesn't like you,' she tried to explain. 'He just doesn't want to get married. Some men don't.'

Immediately, a picture of Jonas popped into her head, although why it had when she hadn't been thinking of him was a mystery. Then again, perhaps it wasn't so mysterious after all. He was the Casanova of the ER, Dr-Footloose-and-Fancy-Free, the only man she knew who considered marriage akin to a case of encephalitis—something to be avoided.

Yet no matter how she tried to focus on his flaws, one simple fact remained. Although he bore some culpability, she'd treated him poorly, taking her anger out on him rather than on the jerk who deserved it.

'You'll still be our mommy, though, won't you?'

'Absolutely. We're family and that makes us a set. Everyone knows you don't break a set.'

Even as she gave that explanation, a fresh feeling of anxiety washed over her. If she became HIV positive, then her reassurances would mean absolutely nothing and once again these two would lose someone close to them. Surely fate wouldn't be that cruel, but she knew there were no guarantees.

Swallowing hard as she pasted a serene look on her face which was purely for the children's benefit, she held the last spoonful of macaroni and cheese to Trevor's mouth.

Fortunately he was too busy clamping his lips together and shaking his head to notice how her hand shook slightly.

With dinner over, she wiped his small face, which was almost a carbon copy of his sister's right down to his pert little nose. Personality-wise, they were very different. Angie led and Trevor followed, although Megan suspected that would change when their interests developed in other directions.

Vowing to fight a potentially grim fate with every fiber of her being, she smiled at him. 'Have you had enough, young man?'

In reply, he pointed to the back yard visible through the glass patio doors and arched his back, as if trying to slide out of his high chair.

'He wants to play in the sandbox,' Angie interpreted.

'Really. I didn't hear him say that.'

Angie shrugged her shoulders. 'He does.'

'He'll never learn to talk if you speak for him.'

'But I know what he wants.'

'Yes, and when you're at preschool, he'll be in trouble because no one else will understand.'

'Oh. OK. I'll try to be quiet.'

Megan knew that Angie had good intentions, but she also understood the close bond between brother and sister. After losing the two most important people in their lives, it wasn't any wonder they'd become inseparable.

'Let me clean Trevor up a bit and then you can play outside.' Her yard was fenced and anything that could cause harm had been relegated to the garage long ago. The window over the sink allowed her to see every inch of their play area, so she didn't mind leaving the two on their own for a few minutes while she washed the dinner dishes.

She carried Trevor to the sandbox and left him happily digging with his shovel while Angie started forming a mound.

'I'll be back out as soon as I'm finished to see what you've built,' she instructed the two. 'Remember. No throwing sand.'

'We won't,' Angie promised.

Megan hurried inside and began running water into the sink. The doorbell rang and, because she wasn't expecting anyone, she dried her hands and went to the front door filled with curiosity.

To her surprise, Jonas stood on the porch. Immediately, the anxiety over her needlestick injury returned with a vengeance and she thought the worst as she opened the glass storm door.

'What's wrong?' She heard the panicky note in her voice and winced at the sound.

He smiled, appearing far too mouth-watering in the jeans that molded every inch of his lower body. His red polo shirt with a logo of a country club on his left breast pocket appeared uncommonly soft and far too touchable for her peace of mind.

He held up a familiar-looking notebook. 'Nothing's wrong. You left this at the hospital and I volunteered to deliver it.'

'You could have called. I was going to run some errands tonight and I could have stopped by the hospital for it.'

'Yeah, but this way you didn't have to.'

Megan stepped aside to allow him in, grateful that for once her living-room floor wasn't completely covered with toys. 'Thanks,' she said as she accepted her property. 'Without this, I'd be lost.'

'I'm surprised you haven't gone the way of technology and bought one of those electronic gadgets.'

She shrugged. 'I'm old-fashioned, I guess. Seeing my schedule on paper is easier.' Realizing she looked a fright, with purple soft-drink stains on her ragged T-shirt, her hair uncombed and a wet spot on her jeans from washing dishes, she wondered what to do next.

'Am I keeping you from dinner?' he asked.

'No. We just finished. The kids are outside and I don't want to leave them unsupervised for long.'

'Then I'll be brief. For what it's worth, I'm truly sorry about how things worked out with you and Dwight.'

Her gaze instantly traveled to the cardboard box filled with Dwight's possessions. Two bestselling hardcover adventure novels, an electric razor, several mugs, a toothbrush and his chess set. Now that she thought about it, she hated chess and had only learned because he'd insisted. She'd also packed every photo she could find, including the frames. It seemed pointless to keep them when she couldn't look back on their time together with fond memories.

All in all, it wasn't much to show for a thirteen-month engagement, but she knew that once his things were out of her house, she'd feel free to move on with her life.

'I didn't put ideas in Dwight's head.'

She moved to the dining-room table where she could talk to Jonas and still keep an eye on Angie and Trevor, still happily playing in the sand.

'You could have encouraged him to work things out. Instead, you persuaded him to call off our engagement.'

'He's been struggling with this for a long time,' he pointed out. 'If he hadn't adjusted to the idea by now, he never would. As for persuading him to call things off, I only convinced him of the timing. For your sake, I thought he should tell you how he felt now, rather than later.'

Megan brushed a lock of hair off her forehead, hating to admit what she suspected in her heart—that Dwight would have ended things with or without Jonas's intervention. She *wanted* to blame Jonas, because it took some of the guilt for their failed relationship off her shoulders, even though he truly wasn't at fault.

Now that it was all said and done, perhaps things had worked out for the best. If Dwight couldn't accept the children, then she didn't want to marry him either. Other women handled being single parents, so could she. In essence, she'd been one for the last year and had managed just fine. More or less.

'You're right,' she said slowly. 'If he'd been having doubts for this long, he always would.' Now that she looked at her circumstances more objectively, she mourned the loss of her dreams far more than she mourned Dwight's absence. Clearly, she didn't love Dwight as much as she thought she did.

'Then you don't think of me as the bad guy?' he teased, but she sensed his underlying earnestness.

'Not really. No.' As she spoke the words, she realized that she meant every one. 'Would you care if I did?'

He paused, as if he hadn't quite worked out the reasons for himself. 'To be effective in the ER,' he said slowly, 'we need to function as a team. We can't be at each other's throats, finding fault and arguing.'

He had a point, although she didn't think it would have come to that. If she did hold a grudge, she would have ignored him, but since she didn't, she wouldn't.

'There won't be any problems on my end,' she reassured him.

'I'm glad.' He flashed one of his megawatt smiles and something stirred deep inside her—something that she refused to name because it would only leave her with heartache. She'd be foolish to let those feelings blossom. Being tired and with her emotions in an uproar, it wasn't any wonder that she was yearning for things she shouldn't.

'I just wish I'd acknowledged the signs,' she said. Talking about Dwight would keep her mind off the spark that had ignited at the most inopportune time. 'I've been thinking about our relationship all afternoon and I can't believe I was so blind. He was so supportive throughout the funeral and afterwards when I brought Trevor and Angie home with me, but once I refused to follow his suggestion and make them wards of the state, he started pulling back.'

'Don't blame yourself.'

'Yes, but I still should have seen this coming,' she insisted. 'I feel as if I didn't know him at all.'

Jonas shrugged. 'Some people are easier to read than others.'

A howl of dismay interrupted the conversation. 'Excuse me,' she said as she flew through the patio doors into the back yard.

'What happened?' she asked Angie, at the same time hauling Trevor out of the sand and cuddling him against her.

'I didn't do nothing,' she protested. 'He hit himself with his shovel.'

Jonas watched Megan run one hand over the little boy's head, clearly inspecting for damage. He didn't see any blood, which was a good sign. The toddler had probably scared himself more than anything.

He knew he should go but the sight of Megan comforting the toddler against her breast drew his gaze like flower pollen drew bees. He could deny it all he wanted, but it didn't alter the truth. He was attracted to this woman in a way that he'd never dreamed possible.

He had no business thinking like this. Megan wasn't the live-for-the-moment type that he normally associated with, but his hormones weren't paying attention to his head. He wanted her in a most elemental way and the blood rushing to a certain portion of his anatomy proved it.

After a few minutes of watching her dry Trevor's tears and kiss the top of his head, he was in pain and thoroughly disgusted with himself. He needed to run, not walk, out of this house.

By the time he reached the front door, Megan had reappeared in the dining room. 'Leaving so soon?'

'Yeah. I, um, don't want to keep you away from the kids. I'll see you tomorrow.'

'I'm not on duty. I worked last weekend so I get the day off.'

'Then I'll see you on Thursday.'

'OK.' She followed him to the door. 'Could you do a favor for me?'

Inwardly he groaned. He could think of one very special favor she could do for him. 'Sure. What is it?'

'Drop this box off at Dwight's house.' She gave his address and directions. 'He won't be home—it's his racquetball night—so leave it on his driveway.'

'The weatherman predicted rain,' he cautioned. 'The clouds were rolling in when I came over. His things could get wet.'

Megan's face became a picture of innocence. 'Life is just full of little trials, isn't it?'

Jonas chuckled. He didn't blame her for wanting to rid her house of anything pertaining to Dwight. As far as he could tell, Dwight might have been willing to put a ring on Megan's finger, but he certainly hadn't given her the love or support she'd so desperately needed.

Although Jonas had trouble in the commitment department—thanks to being shuffled from one home to another while his father had been deployed—the women he dated always knew they could count on him for emotional support, day or night. He suspected that right now Megan needed the latter more than she needed the former, and he was more than happy to oblige.

## CHAPTER FOUR

'HAS anyone seen any notices about a lost golden retriever?' Jonas asked the staff congregated around the nurses' station first thing on Friday morning. After three days of camping in his yard, the dog clearly wasn't ready to find his way home.

'I haven't,' Louise, the thirty-ish, divorced ward clerk replied.

'Neither have I.' Bonnie Reynolds, the other RN in the department, shook her blonde tresses. As far as Jonas could tell, she was good at her job, but at twenty-three she didn't have Megan's experience. Then again, Megan had at least six extra years under her belt.

Megan crossed her arms as she leaned back in her chair. Idly, he wondered if anyone else had noticed her pallor, or if it was a trick of the lighting. 'I take it you've found a dog?' she asked.

The strained note in her voice suggested that her washed-out appearance wasn't due to the fluorescent bulbs.

'Actually, the dog found me. It's a female.'

'Lucky dog.' Bonnie sighed before she winked at him, her invitation obvious.

'What are you going to do?' Gene asked.

Jonas shrugged. 'I was hoping to find its owner and tell him to pick up his pet. The poor thing is half-starved. It's probably been gone for a long time.'

Louise restocked the slots with all the appropriate forms. 'Is it wearing a collar?'

'No, and that's something else I intend to have a few words with his owner about.'

'Uh-oh.' Louise glanced up at him.

'Uh-oh, what?'

'No collar. Half-starved. I doubt if you're going to find anyone to claim him. People dump dogs in the country all the time, or let them off on the interstate.'

Jonas had heard the stories, which only confirmed his own convictions about not keeping an animal. 'That's pretty irresponsible. The least he or she could have done was find a home for it.' Once every single one of his fellow interns had decided to get rid of their pets, they'd each found a family who'd wanted them.

'You'd think so,' Gene agreed. 'But it doesn't always happen.'

'The question is, do you want to keep her?' Louise asked.

Jonas shrugged. It gave him a sense of homecoming when he arrived each evening and found the retriever waiting patiently on his porch, its tail thumping as if it was glad to see him. Yet, like his friend, Joey, he had no business owning a pet. Between his twelve-hour shifts, four to five days a week, and moving around the country, he simply couldn't take on the responsibility.

'To be honest,' he admitted, 'I was hoping she'd leave on her own.'

'Have you fed and watered her?' Bonnie asked.

He already knew what the group would say. 'I had to,' he defended himself. 'She was dehydrated and I could count every rib.'

Louise shook her head dramatically. 'Oh, Dr Taylor, you've gone and done it. She'll never leave on her own now.'

'I've only given her a few leftovers.'

'Food is food,' she said practically. 'I'd say you've made a friend for life. Unless you stop feeding her.'

He'd tried to on Wednesday night, but as dusk had fallen

and he'd seen the dog still waiting patiently by the water dish, he'd surrendered and doled out a few slices of bread along with the contents of his last can of tuna. Then, trying to be firm, he'd left for work on Thursday morning, again without providing breakfast, but the animal's hopeful gaze had lingered in his mind.

Knowing he'd feel guilty all day if he didn't do something, he'd dashed to the hospital cafeteria, bought a mound of eggs, sausage and hash browns and coaxed one of the night shift ER nurses to drop it by his house on her way home.

'I tried, but I can't,' he said.

'There's always the Humane Society,' Gene suggested. 'They'll pick her up, have a vet check her out and make her available for adoption.'

'Don't people usually want puppies instead of adults?'

'That's a risk you take,' Gene pointed out. 'If no one wants her or claims her…' He shrugged again.

Although Jonas knew what happened to those animals, it didn't mean he had to like that scenario. 'What she needs is a good home.'

Megan finally joined in the conversation, still looking pale as every movement she made seemed slow and deliberate. 'So give her one.'

'She needs a place with kids who'll give her attention and love her within an inch of her life. You wouldn't want her, would you?' he asked. 'For your two munchkins?'

'Sorry. No can do. You'll have to find another adoptive family. Or call the Humane Society.'

Bonnie laid a hand on his forearm and smiled a beguiling smile. 'I'll help you look for a good home. No matter how long it takes.'

He grinned, well aware that her invitation included other things than the task she'd volunteered to undertake. She was the sort of woman who didn't ask for more than he was willing to give, the kind who was interested in having a good time until he either left or the next exciting fellow came into her sights. He didn't have any doubts that she could make his stay in Stanton quite interesting.

Surprisingly enough, he wasn't even tempted to accept. Seeing Bonnie and Megan side by side, he knew which woman he wanted and which one he didn't.

'Thanks for the offer,' he said as he flashed Bonnie one of his killer smiles to soften the rejection. 'I think I'll see what luck I have on my own.'

She squeezed his arm—a slow, lingering type of squeeze that was filled with promise and guaranteed to turn a man into a pliable mass. A few weeks ago it would have been effective on him, but not now. The only touch he wanted to experience was Megan's, and from the disgusted look on her face it wouldn't happen any time soon, if ever.

'If you should change your mind, just give me a call.' Bonnie winked. 'Day or night.'

'I will.'

Louise broke into the conversation. 'You do realize that if you're going to give her away, the new owner will want a guarantee that she's healthy. I'm talking vaccinations, de-worming and who knows what else.'

He'd guessed that. Paying for a trip to the vet didn't sound bad if it helped with his ultimate goal of someone taking the retriever off his hands. 'Not a problem.'

'As a dog owner myself,' Gene added, 'you'd better switch to dog food. If they get used to people food, they won't touch the stuff they're supposed to eat.'

'I have a friend who works at the grain co-op,' Bonnie said brightly. 'I'll put in a good word for you. I'm sure he'll give you a discount.'

As Bonnie fluttered her eyelashes, Megan wondered how much longer she could tolerate the other nurse's blatant bid for Jonas's personal attention.

Normally, she welcomed the opportunity for staff to mill around the central nurses' station. It was a time for people to chat, catch up on the latest news or just talk about medical concerns on a more informal basis than in the departmental meeting. Yesterday she'd taken the initiative to mention her broken engagement and had glossed over the reasons with a hearty, 'We decided that we wanted different things in life.'

While she enjoyed these impromptu gatherings, she almost wished they would end. The female staff flocked around Jonas like buzzards on the scent of fresh roadkill and their interest rarely centered on hospital topics. Even Gene, the only other male on this shift, didn't seem to mind the admiration Jonas received.

Too disgusted by the younger nurse's posturing to watch or listen to what would happen next, Megan rose without a word. She'd thought of a few choice comments to make, but talking required more of an effort than she could summon. Last night her stomach had started a perpetual rollercoaster ride and the OTC meds she'd taken hadn't helped. Jonas's warnings about the side effects of the antiretroviral medications had become fact and she could only hope her symptoms would level out before long. She didn't know what she'd do, or how she'd manage, if they became worse.

Intent on putting distance between herself and the crowd that had gathered around Jonas, she walked toward the supply room. Actually, she ambled, because every step seemed to aggravate the churning in her midsection. If fate was kind, Louise's huge white board that showed the patient room assignments would remain empty long enough for her to chew another handful of antacids.

Jonas fell into step beside her. 'Not in the mood to be sociable this morning?'

'It's too early to watch you two drool over each other.'

He clutched a hand to his chest melodramatically. 'Drool? We weren't drooling. At least, I wasn't.'

She raised one eyebrow as she met his gaze. 'You could have fooled me.'

'Bonnie was just being helpful.'

'Yeah, right.' She was used to her colleague's flirtatious ways. Bonnie was known to play the field and Megan wouldn't be surprised if every male in the county under the age of forty had sampled her well-developed charms.

What did bother her, and it shouldn't, was how Jonas seemed to preen under Bonnie's attention. To think she was worried about contracting HIV from a needlestick injury when Jonas should be worrying about that and every other possible disease if he accepted what the other nurse was freely offering.

As she popped the pink tablets in her mouth, she saw the smirk on his face. 'Stop smiling.'

He laughed aloud. 'You're jealous.'

'I am not jealous. Why should I be? If you want to spend your time with Bodacious Bonnie, then—'

'Bodacious Bonnie?'

'Don't tell me that you haven't noticed her cleavage.'

'It's rather impossible not to,' he said in a dry tone.

Of course it was. The younger nurse always wore T-shirts that showed her curves to their best advantage. Thanks to regular exercise and Mother Nature who'd kindly made her well proportioned, Megan wasn't unhappy with her own figure. However, compared to Bonnie, she felt positively shapeless and dowdy.

'Just so you'll know, they're fake.'

Curiosity gleamed in his eyes. 'Really?'

'Yeah, really. Now, if you're through bothering me, I have to check our stock of IV sets.'

'You know,' he commented idly, 'until this week, I thought you didn't have a grumpy bone in your body.'

For a woman who always tried to focus on people's good qualities and overlook the bad, his gentle chastisement hit hard. Normally she was the most even-tempered person, but ever since Jonas had interfered in her life she'd turned into a person she didn't like.

He hadn't interfered, she reminded herself. At least, not to the point where he'd affected the outcome. In all honesty, she should thank him for saving her from certain disaster.

She rubbed the back of her neck. 'I apologize. I just don't…'

'Feel well,' he finished.

Megan stared at him in surprise. 'How did you know?'

'I'm a doctor. I majored in "green around the gills" and, believe me, you have a galloping case of them. So the old stomach is on the warpath?'

'Like you wouldn't believe.' Megan pressed a spot in her middle. 'I've tried the usual over-the-counter remedies, but nothing has worked.'

'I'll prescribe something stronger,' he said. 'If that doesn't help, we'll cut down the dosage of your medications.'

'But won't they be less effective against the virus?'

'Not if you take the same number of milligrams in a day's time. You'll just take them more often.'

'Does that protocol really help the nausea?'

He shrugged. 'For some, yes.'

She wasn't totally reassured. She'd rather discontinue the offending drugs but, given the alternative, she'd take nausea any day. 'Any word from the lab about Carl Walker's Western blot results?'

'No. I thought I'd hear something yesterday, but I didn't, so I'll look into it today. I promise to let you know what I find out.'

'Thanks.'

'Now, why don't we go into the lounge and I'll fix a cup of hot tea? I'll bet I can even find a few crackers.'

Darn it! She didn't want him to be kind or thoughtful, but crackers and tea did sound heavenly. 'Then you know how to boil water?' she teased.

'Two minutes in the microwave,' he said promptly, and put actions to his words while she looked on. 'Don't skip lunch either. Stick to gelatin and chicken soup.'

Jonas was definitely being far too kind for her peace of mind. Right now she had enough on her proverbial plate without adding Jonas to the mix.

Don't be a fool, she chided herself. He's not adding anything to the mix. Preparing tea had been a friendly gesture, nothing more and nothing less. Her weak stomach was making her think all sorts of weird thoughts that were grounded more in fantasy than in reality.

He passed her the steaming cup and she decided that she'd only imagined the way his hands had lingered before he'd let go. 'Take things easy for a few minutes,' he advised. 'Come back when you're ready. If we need you before then, I'll let you know.'

Megan drank most of the tea and ate sufficient crackers to settle her stomach before Gene popped his head inside the room to make an announcement. 'I've got a patient for you, Megan.'

'Who?'

'Mrs Spears. No one else will take her.'

Today Megan didn't want her either, but she didn't have a choice. 'I'll be right there.'

As Megan had suspected, Violet Spears's problem hadn't developed overnight and would take a long time to cure.

'You've had this for quite a while, haven't you, Mrs Spears?' Megan asked as she gazed at the ulcer she'd uncovered on the woman's leg. It was the size of her fist, had an angry-looking core, and from the grimaces on Mrs Spears's face was extremely painful.

The sixty-year-old patient with gray hair that hadn't seen a comb for the last year nodded. 'Don't remember exactly when I noticed it, but it's gotten so I cain't get round town on my bike.'

Violet Spears wasn't unknown in the ER. She arrived from time to time, needing treatment for a variety of ills that ranged from pneumonia to a sliced hand. No matter what the situation, she arrived in the worst-smelling condition imaginable. Although she owned a house, she was for all intents and purposes homeless. According to the social workers, she lived without electricity or heat, except for a fireplace that they were afraid was more hazardous than helpful.

'How's your other leg?' Megan asked as she tugged off the gray sock on Violet's left foot and placed it beside the red one she'd already removed.

'It's fine.'

Megan noticed an area that would probably turn into another ulcer soon if left untreated, but didn't comment. Jonas could decide what to do for this woman who needed help but usually refused it.

'I'm going to get the doctor,' she told Mrs Spears. 'I'll be right back.'

'I ain't goin' nowheres,' the woman answered with a toothless grin.

Megan found Jonas at the nurses' desk, surrounded by staff members waiting for his direction. 'He needs one pill a day for ten days,' he instructed Gene. 'If he isn't better by then, he should see his family physician or visit us again.'

'Will do.'

'Louise,' Jonas called. As the ward clerk turned to him, he said, 'Let me know when Radiology has those X-rays done on the woman in room five. And if we don't have lab results on Mr Lassiter in five minutes, call and remind them that we aren't getting any younger.'

'Sure thing, boss.'

Jonas looked at Megan. 'What do you have?'

She handed over her chart. 'Here's one of our more colorful local characters for you.'

He raised one eyebrow. 'We've already treated a fellow who insists on wearing his clothes inside out and tinfoil on his head and a guy who caught a tender portion of his anatomy in his zipper during a lunchtime liaison with his secretary. Who's more colorful than they are?'

'Mrs Spears,' she answered promptly. 'Have you ever seen a little old lady riding a bicycle around town, carrying a loaded box or trash bag in her basket?'

'Can't say that I have.'

'Well, you will. People have caught her sifting through dumpsters and hauling off anything and everything. This is the lady.'

'Hmm.' He glanced at her record. 'BP is a little high, but not bad. So she has an ulcer on her leg?'

'And the start of one on the other. Good luck.'

'What for?'

'Whenever she's been admitted, she checks herself out AMA,' she said, referring to the 'against medical advice' designation. 'And if she doesn't need hospitalization, unless you can cure her with a single shot, she won't comply with your treatment.'

'Then she drops in quite often?'

'Surprisingly enough, we only see her a few times a year. She's probably built up an immunity to almost every germ and virus on the planet.'

He tucked the clipboard under his arm. 'Then let's see what I can do.'

Megan followed as he entered the room and introduced

himself to the woman sitting on the bed, both dirty legs stretched out on the pristine white sheets. Today was certainly the day for unusual characters. Not many people arrived in the ER wearing a pink sweater with frayed cuffs and holes in the elbows and a dingy yellow T-shirt. Greasy food stains dotted her blue-flowered skirt which, at the moment, was pulled above two dirt-encrusted knobby knees.

Jonas tugged on a fresh pair of latex gloves as he peered at her shins. 'You have cellulitis, Mrs Spears, and it's going to take time to treat it properly.'

Her cloudy gray eyes narrowed. 'Time? How much time?'

'It depends. A few days, maybe a week.'

'I don't have to stay here, do I?' she asked as Jonas began cleaning the wound with the supplies Megan had already set on a tray.

'The dressings have to be changed twice a day. Can you do that at home?'

'I cain't stay here,' she exclaimed.

'Why not? You'll get three meals a day, a warm bed, a bath…'

Mrs Spears shook her head violently. 'Nope. I only gots enough money to pay for today.' She shifted position and pulled a handful of one-dollar bills out of her pocket. 'Ten bucks. Don't have no more to stay longer.'

'The hospital understands if you don't have the money,' Megan said, wondering how she could make the woman understand that they had a legal obligation to provide care regardless of the patient's ability to pay.

Mrs Spears folded her arms. 'Nope. Cain't stay. People will rob me blind if I ain't at home.'

Megan doubted it.

Jonas finished his task and wrapped a dressing around the woman's leg. 'The best place for you to heal is here.

You'll get better so much faster if the nurses can look after you.'

'I kin look after myself.' She pointed to her leg. 'Just finish up what yer doin' and I'll be on my way.'

Jonas glanced at Megan and she shrugged. 'What if I promise to drive by your house every evening?' he asked slowly. 'Just to make sure there aren't any suspicious characters hanging around. Would you stay then?'

Her face gradually lost its mulish set and became more speculative. 'That is an idea.'

Although his willingness to go the extra mile impressed Megan, his offer was fraught with difficulties. No one really knew Mrs Spears's state of mind and if even the smallest blade of grass was disturbed, provided she had any, Jonas could find himself in a heap of trouble.

'You got a good heart, Doctor,' Mrs Spears finally said, 'but I cain't have you doin' such a big thing for me. It wouldn't be right, not when the po-lice won't even drive through the neighborhood 'less they have to. You got enough to worry 'bout with all kinds of sick folk needin' yer attention. I'll just go on home so's I can tend my own affairs.'

'I could ask the police to make extra patrols in your neighborhood.'

Mrs Spears cackled as she met Megan's gaze. 'He don't give up, does he?'

Megan grinned. 'No, he doesn't.'

'I tell you what,' the woman declared. 'I'll come back here twice a day until you tell me I don't need to.'

Jonas stripped off his gloves and shook her bony hand. 'It's a deal.'

Megan doubted if the business office would approve of the arrangement, but if anyone could convince them it was in everyone's best interests, Jonas could.

'Now, if I'm busy or not here,' he warned her, 'one of the nurses will look after you.'

'Fine by me.'

'In the meantime, we're going to give you a couple of shots to jump-start the healing process. You also have to promise that you'll stay off your feet as much as possible and keep them elevated.'

'I expect I can do that,' she assured him.

'Good,' he said as he scribbled his orders on the chart before handing the clipboard over to Megan. 'We'll see you early this evening.'

Megan read his orders for a tetanus injection, antibiotic and thiamine. The woman obviously didn't take vitamins and B1 would help maintain nervous and muscular function in her legs.

Within fifteen minutes Mrs Spears was on her way and promised to return before dark.

'How are you going to justify seeing her twice a day?' Megan asked Jonas as soon as they were alone.

'It's cheaper to slap on a fresh dressing in the ER than to pay for hospitalization,' he told her. 'If we're going to absorb the cost anyway, what will it matter?'

'To me, it doesn't. But the bean counters won't like it. They'll argue that she always sneaks out AMA, so why allow her to tie up ER staff's time, space and supplies?'

He shrugged. 'My way will at least give her a chance at recovery. If we admit her and she walks out, she won't get treated. Plus, I'm hoping that once she builds some trust, we may talk her into staying, at least overnight.'

'I never thought of that,' she admitted.

'What choice do we have? We're potentially looking at septicemia, gangrene and amputation, which is more costly for us in the long run. Bending the rules is worth a try.'

Megan couldn't argue with his logic.

Left alone to ready the room for the next patient, she

was glad she didn't have much to do. Normally the sights and smells of the ER didn't bother her, but they did today. Violet's residual body odor and the pungent smell of her soiled dressings aggravated Megan's already stressed stomach.

The reasons for her nausea reminded her of Carl Walker's pending test procedure. Surely she'd hear something—*anything*—today. When business slowed down to a steady trickle, she'd ask Jonas to call the infection control nurse. She didn't want to take one more of these nasty pills than absolutely necessary.

Jonas returned to his office, wishing the radiologist had given him better news. The elderly gentleman's broken leg wasn't due to his fall but to suspected bone cancer.

And speaking of better news, he had one other woman who was eagerly waiting for an overdue report. He dialed the infection control office number and asked for Susan.

'I was on my way to talk to you,' she told him. 'Is Megan working today?'

'Yes.'

'Could you ask her to meet us in your office? I'll be there in a few minutes.' Before Jonas could agree or ask another question, the dial tone buzzed in his ear.

His gut twisted, although he knew that any HIV test results shouldn't be given over the phone in the interests of confidentiality. Even so, Susan could have said *something* to give him a clue as to what would be forthcoming.

He found Megan where he'd left her, although the tidy trauma room spoke of how hard she'd worked in his absence.

'Susan is on her way to talk to us,' he said without preamble. 'She'll be here shortly.'

Her face brightened. 'She has the results?'

'She didn't say.'

As promised, the fifty-year-old infection control nurse arrived a few minutes later and Jonas closeted himself in his office with both women. With arms crossed and his impassive 'doctor' face in place, he waited for Susan's explanation.

'Megan's baseline results are all negative, as I'd suspected,' Susan began. 'However, we've hit a snag.'

'What kind of snag?' Megan demanded.

Susan appeared apologetic. 'We don't have the Western blot results on Mr Walker yet.'

'Why not?' Jonas asked. 'It should have been done yesterday.'

'I know,' Susan admitted. 'But the lab lost his specimen.'

# CHAPTER FIVE

MEGAN'S pale face whitened another shade. 'They what?'

'How could they lose his blood sample?' Jonas demanded.

'According to the people here, their records show the tube left this lab and arrived at the processing center. The reference lab admits they received it.'

'Then where did it go?' Jonas asked.

'The staff in Nevada are trying to hunt it down. It's somewhere on site, but they don't know exactly where.'

'I still can't believe it,' he said flatly. He knew these large facilities had safeguards in place, but even with them, things happened. Yet it didn't stop him from posing a mental question that he knew wouldn't ever be answered. Why, with the thousands of specimens that were processed, did the one sample they misplaced have to be this particular one?

Megan pinched the bridge of her nose. 'This is just dandy,' she said waspishly. 'So now what do we do?'

'I've been trying to track Walker down,' Susan informed them. 'Then we'll redraw his blood and try this again.'

'I'll admit it isn't the ideal situation,' Jonas said, feeling more calm, although he knew Megan was extremely eager to stop her PEP, 'but we'll only have to wait another few days. Right?'

Susan grimaced as if she didn't like what she had to say next. 'Not exactly. You see, I haven't been able to locate him and I've been trying all afternoon. I finally got in touch with his girlfriend, though.'

'And?' Megan asked.

'Carl hopped on his motorcycle two days ago and disappeared.'

Megan's shoulders slumped and Jonas's own frustration rocketed through the roof. 'She doesn't know where he went? Surely she has a clue.'

Susan shook her head. 'Apparently, he takes to the road when he's upset.'

'Now, *that's* a mature response.'

Jonas didn't blame Megan for being sarcastic. He'd like to find Carl Walker and blister his ears for being so inconsiderate. Didn't he want to know his own test results?

'Some people run from their problems in the hope they'll go away. He clearly fits into that category,' Susan answered.

'Well, bully for him. Unfortunately, some of us don't have that luxury,' Megan snapped.

Jonas didn't blame her for being angry, but it wouldn't help matters. He drew a deep breath and tried to look at the bright side. 'So we have a setback. A time delay. It's not the end of the world.'

Megan's glare would have been comical if the situation weren't so serious. *'We?'* she asked.

'Jonas is right. It isn't the end of the world,' Susan chimed in. 'I'll keep trying to locate him. His girlfriend has also promised to ask him to contact me right away the next time he calls.'

'That could be days. *Weeks.*' Megan's voice rose.

'Not necessarily,' Susan corrected. 'Rae is going to alert his family and friends in case he shows up on any of their doorsteps.'

'The question is, will he call her?' Megan asked.

Jonas exchanged a hopeless glance with Susan. Vanishing into thin air, without telling his significant other, wasn't a positive character trait.

'If he doesn't,' he answered in his most unconcerned

tone, 'it won't matter. We'll continue your prophylaxis for the full month and test you in six weeks, just as we'd planned.'

He watched Megan lower her gaze to study her fingernails and blink several times. When she lifted her head and nodded a few seconds later, her eyes held an unmistakable glimmer.

Something twisted in his heart, and he wished that, in spite of all his knowledge and experience, he wasn't so helpless. He wanted to fix the problem and give Megan a happy ending.

From the way she appeared to draw into herself, he sensed she needed a hug, or at least a shoulder to lean on. He wanted to provide either, preferably both, but with a witness he couldn't.

'I understand,' Megan said quietly, as if she'd come to terms with the latest problem in her current series. 'I'm just not very patient. I had pinned my hopes on being able to DC my meds and forget this had ever happened.'

'A normal reaction,' Susan assured her. 'It's difficult, living with the unknown, but we're doing everything possible for you to have a favorable outcome.' She studied Megan closely. 'Are you experiencing some side effects?'

Megan's smile was wan. 'More than I'd like.'

Jonas broke in. 'I've prescribed something to help lessen the nausea.'

'Good. If you have any other problems, let Dr Taylor know.' Susan rose. 'That's all my information for now. I'll keep you posted.'

'Thanks.'

Jonas stopped Megan on her way out the door. 'Join me for dinner tonight,' he said impulsively.

'What?'

'Dinner. We could try out one of those restaurants you mentioned.'

'Why me?' she asked.

'Why not you?' he countered.

'What's wrong with Bonnie?'

'I don't know. I didn't ask her. So, would you be interested?'

'For starters, I wouldn't be very good company. The way I feel, you'd be wasting your money because the thought of food simply...' She fell silent and shuddered. 'Most importantly, I don't have a sitter.'

'Then how about a movie? I don't know what's playing, but surely we'd find something you liked.'

'I appreciate the invitation,' she said with a small smile, 'but, no, thanks. I'm really not up to going out.'

'What if I brought dinner to you?'

'It's really sweet of you to offer, but I can manage on my own. I don't need help.'

Her face still had its washed-out appearance and, after having her hopes dashed, she looked rather beaten, much like the dog who'd crawled into his yard. If anyone needed help, she did, but he couldn't force her to accept what she didn't want.

'OK, but don't forget to fill my script on your way home.'

'I won't,' she promised.

He should have considered the subject of Megan closed and put her out of his mind after she'd gone home, but he simply couldn't. Sheer determination held her together and he wished that he'd insisted on stopping at the drug store for her. It wouldn't have been any trouble to run the errand and he could have done it more easily than she could with two kids in tow.

'I'll bet she went straight home instead,' he told the dog as it gobbled down the roast beef, mashed potatoes and gravy he'd brought from the hospital cafeteria. He was smarter these days and had started taking home two meals instead of one. If the woman at the checkout wondered about his hearty appetite, she kept her comments to herself.

The retriever licked the styrofoam container clean, then drank about half of its water. Jonas refilled the bowl, then sat on the bottom step, pleased to see the animal now trusted him enough to lie near his feet.

'You'd like her,' he told the dog as he scratched behind her ears. 'She's friendly, smart and, now that I think about it, as stubborn as you are. You're not going home, are you, girl?'

The dog raised its head and licked Jonas's fingers.

'I assume that means no.'

The retriever laid its head on its paws.

'You need a good home. One with kids. You like kids, don't you?'

A soulful gaze met his as its tail thumped several times.

'Don't worry,' Jonas told him. 'I'll find the perfect place for you, but first you're going to need a trip to the vet.'

The animal closed its eyes, as if the conversation had overtaxed its strength.

'Sleep is good,' Jonas said as he straightened to go inside. Megan needed her rest, too, although with two little ones, she probably wouldn't get much.

Suddenly, he simply had to know what was happening at her house. Telephoning wasn't an option—he needed to see for himself that she had everything under control.

Admit it, Taylor, he told himself. You want to be her white knight, riding to the rescue.

Someone had to be, he argued back. She had no one. No family and no fiancé to lean on. It wasn't as if he had anything better to do this evening.

*You could always call Bonnie.*

He dismissed the notion outright. He wasn't in the mood for the Bonnies of the world.

Jonas polished off his own dinner before he returned to

his car. He'd only drop in for a few minutes and see how she was faring. If all was well, he'd come back and find a scintillating program on television. If all wasn't well, he'd deal with that.

He remembered the directions and found Megan's place without any problem. The small yellow-brick house hadn't changed from his last visit, although this time a tricycle lay on its side in the driveway, next to a red wagon. He took time to notice what he hadn't before—the building was a carbon copy of its neighbors with the only real difference being in the color of brick and the shrubbery lining the foundations. In Megan's case, a bright array of tulips and daffodils grew where other people had planted small evergreens.

He righted the trike on his way to the porch and took the steps two at a time. As he raised his hand to poke the doorbell, he heard a childish voice through the open window.

'Trevor broke my wings.'

Megan's soothing voice answered. 'He didn't mean to.'

'But they're my angel wings.'

'I'll fix them.'

'When?' came the demand.

He heard a patient sigh. 'Soon.'

'Are you going to give Trevor a time-out for breaking my stuff? He needs to learn a lesson.'

Jonas grinned at the little girl's tone and listened shamelessly for Megan's reply.

'He's too little to understand. Until he's old enough to know that he has to leave your things alone, you'll need to keep them out of reach. Babies like bright colors, so he wants to see your wings, too.'

'They are pretty, aren't they?'

'Very.'

'Can I go outside and water the flowers now?'

'In a minute.'

Sensing he would be caught if he didn't make his presence known, Jonas pressed the doorbell. A small sprite, dressed in pink pants and a flowered shirt with a Christmas garland on her head and droopy bits of fabric hanging down her back, answered the door.

'Hi,' he said. 'Is your mother, er, Megan here?'

Immediately, Megan appeared behind the child with a toddler on one hip, her short hair tousled. Panic immediately crossed her face. 'What's wrong?'

'Nothing. I wanted to check on you.'

'Since when do you make house calls?'

He smiled inwardly at her suspicion. 'As of today, but only for special patients.'

'I'm not your patient.'

'I prescribed meds for you. In my books, that makes you my patient. May I come in?'

She flipped the inside latch on the handle and stepped aside. 'Things are a mess. I wasn't expecting visitors.'

'Don't worry. I left my white gloves at home.' He stepped inside, noticing how the little girl with curly reddish-gold hair—Angela, he recalled—clung to her leg. The toddler on Megan's hip sported the same color hair, although his was baby-fine and as straight as a backboard. Both watched him with wide-eyed curiosity.

'You could have called,' she said.

'Yes, but this way I can see how you're doing for myself.' He winked at Angela before he glanced at Megan. 'Have you had dinner?'

'I just finished serving the kids.'

'We had bisgetti,' Angela informed him.

That explained the red stain on the front of Megan's faded blue T-shirt. Something else, though, lingered in the air. Something chocolate if his nose was accurate.

'From a can,' Angela added. 'It's not as good as Mommy's, but she's not feeling good.'

'I know. That's why I came.' He looked at Megan. 'Have you eaten?'

'Maybe later.'

'Did you pick up your prescription?'

She turned an endearing shade of pink. 'No.'

'Why not?'

'Trevor was fussy and I wasn't in the mood to stand in the drug store with a crabby baby for twenty minutes.'

'Don't you have a friend who'd do a favor for you?'

'Yes, but Serena is attending a neonatal nursing class for the next few weeks. I'll get the script filled tomorrow.'

'Don't be ridiculous,' he said. 'Most places deliver, so I'll call it in.'

'You're too late. Seven p.m. is their cut-off time.'

'Fine. I'll go after it myself. Where's your phone?'

She pointed to a nook near the dining-room table. 'There.'

'Do you have a store preference?'

'No.'

He flipped through the *Yellow Pages* to find a pharmacy that featured late hours and telephoned his order, promising to arrive before they closed at eight. 'You're all set,' he said after he rejoined her in the living room.

Angela raised her chin to look up at Megan and spoke in a loud whisper. 'Is he a doctor like Dwight?'

'Yes, he is. Dr Taylor works in the emergency room where I do. Jonas, this is Angela, although we call her Angie.' She jiggled the toddler in her arms. 'This bundle of energy is Trevor.'

'I'm pleased to meet you and your brother,' he told the youngster.

Angie smiled shyly, then, as if satisfied by the information and introductions, she released Megan's leg and returned to her *Sesame Street* coloring book on the coffee-table.

'I presume you intend to stay for a while?' Megan asked.

'I came to help with whatever you might need.' He glanced at the remnants of their dinner scattered across the table. 'I'll even wash dishes. I'm an old hand at KP duty.'

'KP? Were you in the service?'

'My dad was. It was just the two of us, so we both took turns in the kitchen.'

'I can manage the dishes,' she told him. 'But since you're here, would you like something to drink?'

'You don't have to wait on me,' he protested.

'Filling a glass with water isn't waiting on you.'

'OK. Water would be great.'

Megan sat Trevor on the floor next to the sofa, then addressed the little girl. 'You can visit with Dr Taylor until I get back.'

'OK.' Angie abandoned her crayons and plunked herself onto the sofa, carefully adjusting her wings so she wouldn't crush them.

Jonas sank into the easy chair in the corner of the room and quickly took note of his surroundings. The house wasn't quite as pristine as it had been on his last visit, but the few toys lying about didn't make the place seem messy. If anything, those things, including a few children's books in a basket next to his chair and the row of photos on a shelf in the bookcase, made the place seem homey.

It was quite unlike his own lackluster quarters. Brightly colored throw pillows covered the nondescript sofa and a quilted wall hanging in shades of green and blue added a cheerful note.

'I'm an angel,' the little girl announced before he could initiate the conversation.

'I see. I like your wings.'

'Trevor broke the wire that makes their shape.'

He bit back his smile at her mournful tone. 'I'm sorry to hear that.'

'My real mommy made 'em, but Aunt Megan's my mommy now and she's going to fix 'em.'

'So your Aunt Megan is good at fixing things?'

'Yeah, but she's not as good as my daddy. Are you a daddy?'

'No, I'm not.'

'Oh.' Before Jonas could wonder what would pop out of her mouth next, she jumped off the sofa and pirouetted in front of him. 'Aren't my wings pretty?'

'They're beautiful.'

'Mommy Megan made me some more. I wear them all the time, especially when I ride my tricycle.'

'Do they help you go fast?'

She nodded. 'Would you like to see how many I have?'

'I'd love to.'

Angie scurried around the sofa and disappeared, presumably into her room. Jonas smiled at her exuberance, wondering how Megan, or any parent for that matter, managed to keep up with such a lively youngster. Idly, he reached into the basket beside him and retrieved a picture book about a little train engine.

Suddenly Trevor's attention drifted to the book in Jonas's lap, then to his face, then back to the book. He started to crawl forward, but abruptly shifted into a sitting position and frowned, clearly torn between his fear of Jonas and his desire to look at his book. Jonas smiled as the little boy's face mirrored his thoughtful dilemma.

Megan's family was like the stray retriever, he decided. They were all leery and somewhat suspicious of him and his motives. Jonas would simply have to show them that he was one of the good guys.

'Is this yours?' he asked softly, holding it up so Trevor could see the pictures.

Without hesitation, Trevor approached Jonas. Using Jonas's denim-clad legs to pull himself upright, he rose, and once his feet were planted firmly beneath him he raised his arms.

Jonas smiled. It didn't require experience to understand what the toddler wanted. 'Do you want to sit with me?'

Trevor grunted and Jonas lifted him onto his lap. The little boy immediately snuggled next to him and pointed to the picture.

Jonas was stunned beyond belief by Trevor's instant trust. How could Dwight have had second thoughts about raising these kids as his own? Had the man lost his mind?

Trevor tapped the picture impatiently and Jonas dropped those thoughts to begin reading the story.

By the time Angie appeared with five pairs of angel wings in an assortment of colors, and Megan returned with glasses of ice water, Jonas was on page five.

He stopped reading as soon as he saw the strangest expression on Megan's face. 'What's wrong?'

'Nothing. I'm just surprised. Trevor won't go to strangers. Why, he wouldn't even sit on Dwight's lap and he's known him for ever.'

Jonas grinned, privately thrilled that he had one advantage over the plastic surgeon. 'I have the touch, I guess.'

Trevor grunted and pointed.

'I think I'm supposed to finish reading.'

Megan smiled. 'You'd better or he'll never give you a moment's peace.'

Several minutes later, Jonas said the magic words, 'The end.' Trevor closed the book and slid down Jonas's leg. As soon as his feet touched the carpeting, he toddled over to Megan and begged to sit in her lap.

A smile broke out on Megan's exhausted face as she hauled the little boy into her embrace. She set him in the crook of one arm and brushed the lightest kiss on his temple as she hugged him close.

Watching Trevor lean against Megan's softness made him realize how provocative a picture it was. He'd seen other friends, other parents, cuddle their children, but those sights hadn't packed the same punch that the one with Megan did.

Angie immediately thrust her angel wings under Jonas's nose and he reluctantly turned his attention to her. 'Aren't they be-oo-tiful?' she crooned.

Her wings came in nearly every color of the rainbow. Each set was made of sheer fabric and decorated with glitter. Some had sequins haphazardly glued on, which added to the wings' sparkle.

'These are the best angel wings I've ever seen,' he told her solemnly. 'You must take good care of them.'

Angie preened under his attention. 'I do.'

'Did you help make them?'

Her head bobbed up and down. 'I sprinkled the glitter.'

'You did a great job.'

'Mommy did most of the work.'

He smiled. 'Then she did a great job, too.'

'Why don't you put them in your closet for safekeeping?' Megan asked. 'It's almost time for your bath and then bed.'

Jonas thought he detected a note of relief in her voice. He carefully placed the revered wings in Angie's arms. 'Thanks for showing them to me.'

'You're welcome.' Angie carefully carried them out of the room.

Megan tickled Trevor's belly. 'Are you ready for your bath?' she asked.

He giggled with delight. 'Baa,' he repeated.

Sensing his cue to leave on his errand, Jonas rose. 'I suppose I've given the pharmacy enough time to process your script. I'll be back soon.'

'I'll leave the door unlocked,' she said. 'In this house, bathtime is playtime and we don't rush.'

A mental image of Megan lounging in a tub and wearing nothing but bubbles made him forget to exhale. At the same time his body seemed to catch fire. If it had been anyone else, he would have followed her statement with a quip or some witty banter. *Conserve water, share a tub*, sprang to mind.

Then, before he could recover from that picture, Trevor fisted the fabric between her breasts to keep his balance as she rose, and Jonas caught a substantial glimpse of creamy skin.

He needed to leave before he totally embarrassed himself.

'I'll yell before I walk in,' he said as he headed for the door.

Driving through town, he willed himself back to normal. His good deed was rapidly turning into something painful, but he couldn't stay away from her any more than he could compete in the Olympics.

At Farley's Drug Store, he handed over the script he'd written for Megan and identified himself to the pharmacist on duty. After a brief conversation, he left with pills in hand.

Back at Megan's house, he was surprised to see Angie sitting on the porch's top step with Trevor on her lap. She wore a pink nightgown, fuzzy pink slippers and white angel wings, while Trevor was dressed in a footed blue sleeper.

'What are you two doing out here?' he asked.

'Mommy made us.'

'Why?'

''Cause our house is on fire.'

# CHAPTER SIX

*STAY calm.*

Megan squinted to see her way through the thick haze. Her stove was smoking like a chimney as it devoured the cupcakes she'd been baking. It was bad enough that her kitchen, dining room and living room were filled with a gray fog, but if Angie hadn't gone to the living room to choose a bedtime story book and run back to report this unusual event when she had, the damage could have been far worse.

She clicked off the oven, wondering if that would be of any value at this point, and rummaged through the lower shelf of her pantry for the fire extinguisher.

It wasn't there.

Wait. She'd moved it during her last major house-cleaning to the cupboard beside the stove. Her eyes burned and filled with tears from the irritants in the air and she coughed.

She should have called 911, she thought as her fingers closed around the handle and she hauled it out of its storage place. Before she could release the pin and aim the nozzle of her ABC fire extinguisher inside the oven, large hands covered hers and a deep voice filled her ears.

'Get out.'

'This is my house and my fire. I'll take care of it.'

'No, you won't.' He grabbed the extinguisher from her hands. 'Call the fire department and stop arguing. Now, get back!'

Immediately Jonas pulled the pin, aimed the nozzle as he inched open the door and squeezed the trigger. Foam shot inside, covering the burning mass of what once had been cupcakes. She didn't think cake could catch fire, but obviously, as the food burned, the paper liners had burst into flame.

Realizing there was little else for her to do, she hurriedly placed the call, then ran outside to see that Angie and Trevor were exactly where she'd left them.

'Everything's fine,' she told the pair. 'Just sit tight for a few more minutes.'

'My angel wings,' Angie wailed.

'They're OK.' Megan went back inside and opened every window to help rid the place of smoke. She returned to the kitchen and found Jonas standing in front of her stove with white foam dripping onto his shoes.

'What are you doing in here?' he demanded.

'Trying to clear out the smoke. Surveying the damage.'

He pointed to the white-covered mass. 'Whatever those were, I don't think you're going to be serving them.'

She heaved a sigh. She could have saved herself all sorts of trouble if she'd just stopped at the store on her way home from work. But, no, Angie had wanted home-made goodies and nothing else would do.

'Those were chocolate cupcakes for Angie to take to day care tomorrow. Everyone was supposed to bring something to share at their picnic.'

'Unless she's going to contribute charcoal, I think she'll have to take something else.'

Megan wanted to smile at his humor, but didn't have the energy. A siren screamed in the distance and all she could focus on was how much she dreaded the next few hours.

Hours, heck. The next few days, not to mention *weeks*, would be another load on her over-burdened shoulders.

'We'd better go outside,' she said wearily.

She hadn't reached the door before Trevor's shrill cries joined the sirens. The second her feet hit the porch, he held out his arms and his cries turned into hiccups.

'Were you scared?' she soothed as she took him from Angie's hold. He sniffled and she wiped away the trail of tears on his cheeks, realizing she was leaving soot on his face. She wasn't in the best shape to hold a freshly bathed baby, but if being in her filthy arms calmed him down, then so be it.

What she wouldn't give for a trip to the bathroom. Her eyes still burned and she probably had as many, if not more smudges on her face than Jonas sported on his.

She moved Trevor to one hip and caught a whiff of herself. The odor of smoke nearly made her gag. 'My clothes are ruined.'

'Probably.'

She glanced at Jonas. 'I owe you a new outfit.'

He shrugged. 'We'll see.'

Megan started to argue, but Angie tugged on the hem of Megan's shirt. 'I wasn't scared,' she reported matter-of-factly.

Vowing to revisit the subject with Jonas at a later date, Megan looked at her daughter. 'You weren't?'

The youngster shook her head, then inclined it in Jonas's direction. 'Nope. 'Cause *he* was here.'

Megan glanced at the man who, in the space of an hour, had added another member to his already huge fan club. It was irritating to know that Angie had succumbed so easily to his charm. Not only did dogs and women fall at his feet, but children as well.

What added insult to injury was how she, too, found it comforting to have Jonas beside her as a fire truck and two police cars rolled into the street. One police car blocked the intersection so other traffic couldn't enter, the other parked near her house and the fluorescent yellow fire truck stopped in front of the city's water hydrant not far away. Their red and blue flashing emergency lights were like beacons in the growing darkness.

Men spilled out of the truck, all clad in typical firefighter's gear of yellow reflective striped jackets, rubber pants, black boots and yellow helmets. Several began unrolling hose from the truck while others prepared to hook one end to the water supply.

Three fireman rushed to the porch, the lead man presumably being the captain of this crew.

'It was the stove,' Jonas reported. 'As far as I can tell, the fire's out. Fortunately, we had an extinguisher.'

The captain acknowledged Jonas's report with a nod. 'We'll check it out to be sure.' He spoke into his walkie-talkie to someone near the truck and the activity on their end came to a halt.

As the three disappeared inside, Megan's adrenaline rush faded, leaving her with a stomach that wanted to turn itself inside out. It didn't help to have to go through the story with the police officer for his report. He wrote down everything, including her name, address, phone number, insurance company and employer.

By the time he snapped his little notepad closed, Megan was totally drained. She sank onto one of the plastic lawn chairs she'd purchased last summer and closed her eyes to the neighbors gathering under the streetlamp.

'I feel like such an idiot. I can't believe I forgot to set the timer.' By the time she'd gotten home, she'd no longer functioned at peak efficiency and she'd known it, which was why she'd resorted to serving canned spaghetti. In fact, she'd been operating at fifty per cent, and it was obvious that that level wasn't good enough. She had two children depending on her and she couldn't afford to make such simple mistakes.

'I'm sure you're not the first person who's cremated cupcakes,' Jonas said dryly. 'And I doubt if you're the last.'

'That makes me feel better.'

Captain Rucker, according to his sewn-on name tag, joined them on the porch with his men. 'Everything's clear. We took what was left of your pan into the back yard.

Before you replace your stove, you should have your electrician check the wiring. You basically have smoke damage, but it's not bad. A good cleaning service should take care of that.'

'Thanks.'

The men headed down the steps, but the captain stopped at the bottom. 'Oh, and one more thing.' His eyes held a definite twinkle. 'Be sure and recharge your extinguisher.'

'She will,' Jonas answered.

As soon as the vehicles started down the street, the small crowd of neighbors advanced. 'Oh, dear,' Megan muttered under her breath. 'Here they come.'

'This is probably the most excitement these folks have seen in a long time,' he answered.

'Yeah, well, I wish someone else had provided them with their cheap thrill.'

'On the bright side, you'll only have to tell your story once. Who's the ringleader?'

'Mrs Ostwell. My next-door neighbor. The one who complains if Angie runs across her yard.'

'I assume she's also the block's center of information?'

'Chief gossip and tale-bearer,' she agreed, pasting a smile on her face just as the seventy-year-old lady marched up the driveway.

'My goodness, dear. What happened?'

'Megan had some problems with her oven,' Jonas supplied. 'The captain suggested that she check out her wiring.'

Megan glanced at him, too surprised to contradict him and too grateful to try. He'd told just enough of the truth to satisfy their curiosity without painting her as incompetent.

'That's too bad.' Mrs Ostwell clucked her tongue. 'Can't be too careful with appliances these days. It's a good thing you were home when it happened.'

'Absolutely,' Megan choked out as she met Jonas's gaze.

'If you'll excuse us,' Jonas said, 'we need to get the children indoors. I'm sure you wouldn't want them to become ill in the night air.'

'Oh, no. Not at all.' Mrs Ostwell and her cronies backed away. 'If you need any advice, you just call on me.'

*Not likely*, she thought. 'Thank you, I will,' Megan replied instead. 'And thanks for being so concerned about us.'

'Goodnight,' Jonas added, and immediately ushered them into the house.

The acrid scent of smoke seemed stronger than before and Megan's stomach protested vehemently. Try as she may, this time she couldn't will the churning to stop. Gritting her teeth, she thrust Trevor at Jonas and bolted for the bathroom.

Jonas stared at the little boy who clearly wasn't sure about this sudden development. In fact, Jonas was certain the toddler would object most vehemently but, oddly enough, after Trevor stared at him, the indecision in his eyes disappeared. He flung one arm around Jonas's neck and laid his head on Jonas's shoulder.

Jonas froze. The children he usually saw were either too sick to fight him or just sick enough to be frightened to death of the man who poked and prodded their small bodies. Trevor's instant faith in him was humbling and at the same time both scary and awesome.

'He's tired,' Angie said importantly.

'I guess so. Shall we put him to bed?'

'Trevor eats a snack first.'

'OK. What kind of snack?'

'Mommy mixes up some oatmeal for him. His milk is in the 'frigerator. Is she sick?'

Retching sounds drifted down the hallway. 'Her stomach is upset, but she'll be better soon.'

'Oh.' Angie wrinkled her nose. 'Want me to show you where Trevor's food is?'

The soft, steady breathing in Jonas's ear and the limp arms and legs dangling in his embrace suggested that Trevor was already out for the count. 'I think we're too late. He's asleep.'

Angie stood on tiptoe to see. 'Yup, he is,' she whispered. 'I'll show you where his bed is.'

'Good idea.'

Jonas followed her down the hallway to a small room with a crib. He placed Trevor on the mattress and covered him with a comforter dotted with frolicking lambs. Angie snapped on the small lamp that served as his nightlight.

'Now it's your turn,' he told her.

Angie led him to her room where a border featuring angels of all shapes and sizes circled the ceiling. She pulled back the pink gingham comforter and crawled underneath. 'Mommy usually reads us a story before we go to sleep.'

Knowing the ritual was an important part of her bedtime routine, he nodded. 'Do you want to choose one or should I?'

'I will.' She leaned over to her nightstand and grabbed a small book that was well worn. Since Jonas was eager to check on Megan, he was glad to see that he could easily read it in five minutes.

'OK,' he said, sitting on the edge of her bed. 'Let's read about Bert and Ernie.'

Five minutes later he turned the last page, but Angie's eyes were still wide. 'I can't sleep. My room smells funny.'

The smoke had clearly infiltrated into this part of the house, although the odor wasn't as strong as in the main living areas.

'Try to relax while I talk to Megan and see what we can do. OK, half-pint?'

She giggled at his name. 'Half-pint? What does that mean?'

He grinned. 'It means you're a little person and someday you'll grow into a lovely lady like your mother. Now, close your eyes and think happy thoughts while I check on your mom.'

'OK.'

Jonas found Megan standing near the phone as she studied the *Yellow Pages*. 'Feeling better?' he asked, turning a chair backwards to straddle it.

'If you're asking me if I found instant relief from the pills you brought, the answer is no. If you're asking me how I feel about all this—' she waved her hands in an all-encompassing motion '—the answer is still no. Are the kids asleep?'

'Trevor is, but Angie isn't. Her room smells funny. Her words, not mine.'

Once again, her shoulders seemed to slump. 'I'd hoped the smoke and extinguisher fumes hadn't drifted into the bedrooms.'

'It did, but it's not as bad. Did you call your insurance agent?'

'He'll stop by in the morning. He suggested a motel for the night.'

'Good idea.'

'The only problem is, with the car races this weekend and a special country and western concert, there aren't any vacancies.'

'Is there someone else you can stay with?'

She shook her head and he remembered that her closest friend was out of town.

'What about your parents?'

'They have an apartment in an assisted living complex. It's barely big enough for the two of them.'

'What about your neighbors?'

She gave him a you've-got-to-be-kidding look. 'After meeting the group, what do you think?'

'Sorry I asked.'

She stared into the kitchen and her voice sound far-away. 'What a mess.'

'Yeah, but it could be worse.'

'I know.' She let out a long, heartfelt sigh. 'I truly am grateful my house didn't burn to the ground. I'm just having trouble coping with this on top of everything else.'

Moisture glimmered in her eyes and she brushed at her cheeks, leaving tell-tale streaks. Her lack of control was probably as upsetting as the events themselves.

'Most people would,' he said. 'Myself included.'

'The sad thing is, I don't know where to begin. It's all so *overwhelming*.'

Jonas didn't hesitate. He flung one arm around her stiff shoulders. 'Sure it is, but a week from now you'll look back and laugh.'

Her eyes shimmered as she looked at him and tried to smile. 'Do you think so?'

'Without a doubt.' As he stared at her trembling lips and enjoyed the softness of her body in his embrace, only one thing popped into his head.

*Kiss her.*

Before he talked himself out of his impulse, he closed the distance between his mouth and hers.

It occurred to him as he held her in his arms that none of his previous experiences had prepared him for this one with Megan. Time stood still as he carefully and thoroughly plundered her mouth. With one hand he molded her to him, noticing that she fit his frame like a glove.

In spite of the residual smoke on their clothing, he could still detect traces of her fruity perfume and knew he would never be able to eat apples again without thinking of her.

A sigh escaped her mouth and he quickly took advantage of her parted lips to insert his tongue and caress hers. He stroked her face and traced a path down to her heart. Although he wanted to explore further, a plaintive voice from across the room stopped him.

'I can't sleep,' Angie whined as she tottered down the hall, carrying a teddy bear. 'My nose keeps tickling.'

Megan broke out of Jonas's hold as if propelled by rocket fuel, and all he could think about was Angie's bad timing and his own thwarted desire.

She met Angie halfway. 'I know it's hard, honey, but you'll just have to do your best. Would a fan help?'

The high note in her voice suggested that she wasn't as unaffected as she appeared, and it was a heady thought to realize that she'd felt the impact as much as he had.

'Then I'll be cold,' she said.

'Not if you snuggle under your covers,' Megan answered.

Becoming entangled in Megan's small family had never been his intent, but he couldn't possibly turn his back on them in their hour of need. 'There is another option,' he said slowly.

Megan turned to face him. 'Which is?'

'Come home with me.'

'With you? You're kidding.'

'I'm not.' Now that he'd offered, he realized how much he liked the idea. To a man who thrived on new experiences, this was certain to become a memorable occasion. 'I have a spare room and we can make a pallet for Trevor on the floor.'

'Yes, but...' She hesitated.

'But what?' he coaxed.

She lowered her voice. 'I can't stay at your house.'

'Why not?'

'You kissed me.'

'I'd do it again, if you'd let me, but kisses are a separate issue. I'm offering my house with no strings attached.'

She nibbled on her lip. 'Won't we cramp your style?'

'I'll have to cancel the orgy I had planned but, hey, what the heck. It's all in a good cause.'

Megan blushed. 'Really, Jonas...'

'I wouldn't have offered if your presence would pose a problem,' he said quietly. It would, but the problem was with him, not her. He probably wouldn't close his eyes all night because of Megan lying in the other room in the spare double bed.

'Please, Mommy?' Angie begged. 'Teddy and I would sleep really good.'

Sensing Megan would refuse, he said idly, 'Tell me, something. Do you have trouble accepting help from everyone, or is it just me?'

Her smile was weak. 'Both. We truly won't be in your way?'

'Not at all. Tomorrow is Saturday, so you'll have all day to deal with insurance agents, cleaning services and appliance stores.'

She slapped the heel of her palm to her forehead. 'I forgot. I'm supposed to work tomorrow. It's my weekend.'

'Under the circumstances, I don't think anyone would fault you for taking a personal day. Why don't I call right now and explain? That will give your supervisor the rest of the evening to find a replacement.'

He expected an argument but luckily none came. 'OK,' she said. 'Let me pack a few things first.'

Thirty minutes later, her mini-van—he chuckled inwardly at the irony when he saw it—was loaded with changes of clothes for all three, Trevor's diaper bag filled with his necessities and another bag with his cereal, juice and milk, since Jonas admitted that he didn't have any of the latter.

Megan followed Jonas in her vehicle and once Angie caught sight of the dog standing guard at the foot of his porch steps, she could hardly wait for Jonas to open her door. 'What's his name?' she asked.

'I don't know. She's a stray,' Jonas answered as he loaded himself down with Megan's belongings while she carried a still-sleeping Trevor.

She skipped alongside him. 'Can I play with her?'

'Tomorrow,' Megan said firmly. 'Right now, it's bedtime for little girls and dogs.'

'OK. Goodnight, doggie.' Angie walked into Jonas's house. 'Where's our room?'

'Right here.' Jonas led the way to the second door on the left and dumped their cargo on the bed. 'The bathroom we just passed is yours. Help yourself to the towels, soap and shampoo.'

'Thanks.'

He found an extra bedspread in the hall closet and folded it into a makeshift mattress. Megan laid Trevor on it and covered him with his own blanket while Angie insisted on goodnight kisses from both adults before she crawled into the bed.

'This is much better,' she whispered. 'Teddy and I can sleep now.'

'Sweet dreams,' Jonas said as he watched Angie burrow under the comforter. Trevor snuffled in his sleep, and Jonas knew that if he lived to be a hundred, he'd never forget the picture of innocence sheltered within this room.

'Goodnight, Jonas,' Megan said softly, breaking his concentration.

'Yeah. See you in the morning.' He backed out and closed the door, awed by this new experience. For a man who worked hard at his job and played equally hard at whatever endeavor captured his current fancy, having three guests, two of them under the age of five, made him feel as if he'd started playing a new game but without the rule book.

It's only for one night, he told himself as he trod softly into the living room and turned the television volume to a barely audible level. He tried to forget that he'd offered a roof and a bed to three people who needed one, but the feel of Angie's arms around his neck and her soft kiss on his cheek was indelibly marked in his mind. If that weren't enough, the water running in the shower made forgetting their presence an impossibility.

How he would like to join Megan for a few hours.

Wishing was one thing, reality another. Even if she was willing and the opportunity presented itself, nothing could happen. 'No sex' was part of his prescription and that was that.

But all this, including his memory of their kiss, didn't stop his imagination from running amok.

Not eager for a frigidly cold shower, he refocused on Trevor and Angie and smiled as he remembered how easily they'd declared him trustworthy by their simple actions.

Parenthood *was* an adventure, if the stories his friends had related were any indication. Angie would break hearts and Trevor would attract girls with his big brown eyes and special smile. Yes, it would be interesting to see these two in about fifteen years.

Fifteen years. He never thought ahead that far—it was against his rule. Somehow, though, Megan had totally turned his life upside down and made him forget the very precepts that governed his life.

That wasn't the only rule he'd broken either. He'd always avoided his current flame's family members without exception. Sunday dinners, holiday gatherings, weddings— whatever the occasion, he refused to join in. He knew what would happen if he ever met parents, grandparents, brothers and sisters, but he'd never lumped children in that category.

He had a feeling that he would pay dearly for his mistake.

'My gosh, Megan,' Serena McAllister said as soon as Megan had finished her recitation of the week's events over the phone on Saturday. 'I leave town and all these interesting things happen to you.'

'Some of them I could definitely live without,' Megan replied wryly. 'Like my needlestick injury.'

'I know you're worried about it, but you're doing everything possible to protect yourself. Hang onto that thought.'

'I'm trying.'

'As for Dwight, I say good riddance.'

Megan twisted the telephone cord. 'I thought you were happy for me when he proposed!'

'I was, because he was what you wanted, although I never understood what you saw in him.'

'I wish you'd mentioned something sooner.'

'Are you kidding? Who was I to question if you two could have made a marriage work?'

'You're my friend,' Megan reminded her. 'You're *supposed* to be my voice of sanity.'

'OK. I solemnly promise that the next time you hook up with a self-centered snob, I'll bluntly tell you. Satisfied?'

Megan smiled. 'Yeah.'

'So tell me about this new doctor. The one who invited you to stay at his house last night.'

'There's nothing to tell.'

'Puh-leeze.'

'I hardly know him,' Megan protested mildly. 'Other than he's in his mid-thirties and has lived and worked all over the country.'

'Does he have a significant other? Scratch that. If he did, he wouldn't have invited you to spend the night.'

'Jonas is the type of guy who doesn't have any trouble finding female companionship,' Megan answered. 'He should have been in the navy, because I'm sure he has at least one girlfriend in every port.'

'Is he good-looking?'

'There isn't a woman alive who wouldn't love to be seen with him,' she said wryly.

'That good, huh?'

'Definitely. Before you get any ideas, you should know that he's totally scared of commitment.'

'What makes you say that?'

'He doesn't stay anywhere long enough to grow roots.'

'Maybe he's just not found the right place to call home.'

'Only because he's not looking. To be honest, I don't understand why he's bothering with me and my problems, unless he's doing it out of guilt.'

'He did you a favor when he gave Dwight that advice,' Serena said firmly. 'Otherwise you two would be forever hanging in limbo.'

'I know. The fact remains, I'm not Jonas's usual good-time girl, so why he keeps coming around is a mystery.'

Then again, if Jonas had noticed how the stars had fallen and the earth had stood still during their kiss, perhaps his constant presence in her life wasn't so mysterious after all. She'd been so bowled over by the current flowing between them that her knees had wobbled and her toes had tingled. If he hadn't pressed her against him, she wouldn't have been able to stand.

He'd literally taken her breath away and if not for Angie's interruption, it was hard to tell what would have happened next.

Whatever it was, it would have been so, so sweet.

'You'll be surprised how many men will come around now that dorky Dwight is out of the picture,' Serena commented.

The mention of Dwight's name brought Megan out of her dreamy state. Had the smoke totally fogged her brain? Sure, it was nice, better than nice, to lean on Jonas. He made her feel as if she wasn't standing alone against the world. Yet she had absolutely no business getting dewy-eyed over him.

First of all, she wasn't ready to start another relationship so soon after her fiasco with Dwight, much less have one with a man who would be here today and gone tomorrow. Secondly, she had children to think of, children who needed adults they could count on for the long haul. Jonas didn't fit that most important requirement but, oh, how she wished that he did!

'It wouldn't matter, because I'm not interested,' Megan said flatly. 'And if I was, how many do you think will come around if my HIV test is positive?'

'Now, don't go borrowing trouble.'

'I'm being realistic,' Megan said flatly. 'I need to focus my energies on making a plan for the kids.'

Dead silence. 'You're really spooked by your needle-stick, aren't you?'

'Wouldn't you be?'

She heard Serena's sigh. 'I guess, but you can't think like that. It's self-defeating.'

'I'm only trying to be prepared.'

'But the result could be negative and if it isn't, it could be years before you develop any symptoms. By then—'

'Trevor and Megan will be teenagers. Who knows what shape my father will be in?'

'And we could get hit by a car tomorrow,' Serena declared. 'I, for one, am not going to dwell on the worst-case scenario. The best way for you to do that, too, is to relax and concentrate on the here and now for the next few weeks. The future will take care of itself. As for your love life, who knows? You could discover that your Jonas is a "keeper".'

He might be, Megan admitted to herself, except that he didn't want to be 'kept'. He wasn't even willing to own a *dog*, for heaven's sake. Falling for another man who thought commitment and family responsibilities were horrible fates would rank as one of the most foolish things she could ever do.

And yet...she'd seen the longing on his face before he'd left the bedroom, the soft expression as he'd gazed upon Trevor sleeping on the pallet he'd made and his surprised but pleased expression when Angie had insisted on giving him a goodnight kiss.

Perhaps there was hope for him.

'Speaking of your munchkins, how are they?'

Megan grinned, remembering how she'd woken this morning to the sound of Trevor talking to himself as he'd played with his toes. 'They're great. It was quite an adventure for them to stay at Jonas's house. I was pleased they were on their best behavior at breakfast.'

'How you intend to get any work done today with them underfoot escapes me,' Serena said in a manner that suggested she was shaking her head.

'Fortunately, they're not here. I took them over to my mom and dad's. I'll pick them up around dinnertime.' She hoped she'd finish earlier. With her father as unsteady as he was, she hated to burden her mother with two energetic children for hours on end. It was one thing to be there with them, taking care of their needs so that her parents could shower them with attention, but it was quite another to dump more responsibility on her mom.

'How's your dad?'

'Some days better than others.'

'Did you tell them about what's been going on?'

'Everything except my accident at work.' The news of the kitchen fiasco had bothered them more than hearing about her broken engagement.

'I know you're devastated.' Her mother had said, patting her hand. 'But things will get better. Dwight simply wasn't the man for you. I'm rather relieved that you two realized it before you went through a marriage ceremony.'

Megan had been glad they'd taken the situation in their stride, but it bothered her that they had seen a flaw in his character that she had not.

'Oh, gosh, look at the time. I hate to run,' Serena said, 'and I'm sorry to hear about your house. If I didn't have a roommate, I'd give you the key to my place in a heartbeat.'

'I know. We'll be fine. Thanks anyway.'

Realizing how fast the morning was disappearing, Megan

began airing out the house as she went through her mental checklist of people she'd contacted.

The insurance agent had been helpful and instructed her to save all her receipts for repairs. The cleaning service was more than happy to take on the job of restoring her kitchen and home after the offending stove had been removed. Unfortunately, they weren't available until Wednesday.

Although Jonas had insisted they could stay with him until then, she couldn't justify doing so.

'At least stay one more night,' he'd told her. 'Why stress the kids' lungs when you don't need to?'

With that final argument, she'd reluctantly agreed.

And so, after a quick breakfast of toast and cereal at his house, Jonas went by the rental shop and met them at her address with his blue convertible loaded with fans of every size and shape imaginable. He'd stayed long enough to set them up in each room before going on his golf date. A date that Megan wanted to ask about, but didn't. Sharing a kiss didn't give her the right to ask questions about who shared his spare time.

She still wanted to know.

Determined to keep her mind off Jonas's golf game, she began to clean Trevor's room. It was strange how such simple activity tired out the body while it allowed the mind to run in every direction.

And every direction pointed to Jonas.

Letting him occupy her thoughts was ridiculous. He might be helping her through this weekend's bad patch, but after a few days of Angie's incessant questions and the demands of a toddler he'd be more than happy to walk away from her small family.

Deep down she didn't want him to walk away, but facts were facts. Leopards didn't change their spots and Jonas wasn't the settling-down type. Any man who kissed like he did wasn't going to be satisfied with one flavor when he could have dozens for the asking.

Come Monday morning, her life would return to its pre-Jonas days of work, friends, her parents and her children. Minus Dwight, of course. After this weekend's fiasco was straightened out, Jonas would simply be another colleague, like Gene.

With that issue resolved in her mind, she tackled her chores. Everything washable was washed, including curtains, bedding and clothes. By the time she'd finished wiping down the surfaces, it was three o'clock and she'd missed lunch.

It had been well worth it, Megan decided as she inhaled the fresh clean smell instead of the faint but cloying scent of charcoal. Perhaps if she worked into the evening, she'd get Angie's room in order, too, and they wouldn't have to rely on Jonas's generosity.

The doorbell rang and her heart eagerly skipped a beat at the prospect of seeing Jonas again. Half-annoyed with herself for reacting like a teenager, she purposely ignored her reflection in the hallway mirror. She wouldn't let it be said that she was trying to impress him. He could see her as she was, dirty and disheveled.

'Come in,' she called out as she strode toward the open door. 'You're early.'

Jonas's wide grin made her heart skip a beat. 'I know.'

'Why?'

'Because we have dinner reservations for eight o'clock.'

# CHAPTER SEVEN

'DINNER reservations?' Megan's shock soon gave way to a host of other emotions, with excitement at the top of the list.

'Dinner reservations,' Jonas said firmly. 'At the West Ridge Country Club.'

'We can't go there.'

'Why not?'

'It's frightfully expensive.' She'd always wanted to eat at the club, but it was so far out of her league that she never allowed herself to consider it.

'Regardless, that's where we're going.'

'But what about the children? They can't go to a place that elegant.'

'Which is why I found a babysitter. Jennifer Millard. According to her father, she's sixteen, great with kids and has an opening for this evening. She's coming to my place at seven-thirty so if you have any objections, you'd better say so now.'

Megan had heard of the girl, although she'd never been able to book her because she seemed to be everyone's first choice for a responsible sitter. 'She's fine but, Jonas, this is so unexpected!'

He smiled. 'Sometimes the best times are those that come on the spur of the moment.'

'But to find a sitter, much less Jennifer! You must have been working on this all day.'

'Not really. I met her her father on the golf course today, and when he started telling me about his kids, I got the idea. Fortunately, everything fell into place.' His expression grew serious. 'The question is, do you want to go or have I overstepped my bounds?'

His momentary uncertainty was endearing. For him to have planned everything, down to finding a babysitter, which was a near-impossible feat on such short notice, he obviously knew how to counter any objections she might have.

Maybe she was foolish, but she didn't have to weigh her answer.

'I'd love to go,' she said simply.

The tension on his face eased and his slow grin reappeared. Suddenly, as if he realized the house seemed far too quiet in spite of the whirling fans, he glanced around the room. 'Where are Angie and Trevor?'

'At my parents'. I need to go for them before long. I promised Angie we'd stop at McDonald's on the way home.' She sighed, wishing she'd accomplished more than she had. 'I'd hoped to finish her room, too, but I haven't even started.'

'There's always tomorrow,' he said.

'True.' Perhaps she should have declined his dinner invitation. She had enough work to keep her busy for the next forty-eight hours, and who knew how Trevor and Angie would behave for a sitter they'd never seen before?

Plus, going out to dinner seemed a lot like a date. Although this was a nice gesture, now that she'd let herself think past her initial impulsive desires, she was afraid that subconsciously she would put far more importance on it than she should. On the other hand, spending an entire evening alone with Jonas, without children or their profession to provide a buffer, was so very tempting...

Jonas could see her indecision reflected in her eyes and in the way she chewed on her lower lip. Perhaps he should let her change her mind but, after seeing her initial excitement, he simply couldn't. She needed this evening to realize that she was more than just a mother and a nurse. She was an attractive woman who deserved some time for herself and, by golly, he was going to see that she got it!

'It's only dinner,' he said. 'Not dancing until dawn.'

She nodded and he could see her uncertainty disappear. 'You're right.'

'Then it's settled,' he said, pleased at the prospect of spending a few hours alone with her. 'Why don't you go for the kids and I'll meet you at my house around seven?'

'OK.' Unfortunately, fate, in the form of a dead battery, ruined his plan.

'All right,' he said, after dropping the hood of her minivan and brushing off his hands. 'We'll buy a battery and install it. Then you can pick up the kids.'

'The auto shop isn't far from their house,' she said. 'Would you mind if we did both at the same time?'

He couldn't refuse what was in essence a logical request. Inwardly, he bemoaned the fact that he would be breaking another one of his rules, but it couldn't be helped. 'OK,' he said.

The experience of meeting Megan's parents wasn't as bad as Jonas had envisioned. Her mother, Nancy, was a graceful woman in her early sixties and her father, Dean, was a handsome man, although Parkinson's disease had clearly taken its toll. His speech was slurred but not unrecognizable if one took the time to listen carefully. Although he remained in his wheelchair, his gaze followed his grandchildren's every move. Clearly, the man would have liked to have played with them, but his health simply prevented it.

As for his own reception, they greeted him warmly but didn't ask a multitude of questions. The only tense moment came when Megan disappeared into the bathroom to change Trevor's diaper, but his fears of being grilled to death were unfounded.

'I'm so glad that Megan has someone to rely on,' Nancy told him. 'She takes too much on her shoulders because she doesn't want to worry us.'

He'd suspected as much, and said so.

'You have my thanks, too,' her father managed to say. 'I wish I could do more, but...' He raised one hand helplessly.

Jonas felt the man's frustration. How difficult it would be to be trapped inside one's body, unable to look after one's own family.

'I'm happy to help,' he told them, impressed by their spirit and touched by their obvious concern for their daughter and grandchildren. 'I'll be honest, though. She doesn't like to depend on anyone other than herself.'

Nancy smiled. 'You noticed?'

'Yes.'

'How long have you been in town?' she asked.

'A few weeks. I'm only here to finish out a colleague's contract for a few months.' He felt it necessary to warn them that he wouldn't be a permanent Stanton resident.

'Doesn't matter,' Dean said in his soft, halting voice. 'You're here now. I don't have any right to ask you to help my daughter, but if you can do what you can for her, I'd be indebted. This damn disease!'

Nancy patted his arm in an obvious attempt to soothe his frustration. 'It's all right, Dean.' Then, addressing Jonas, she added with a gentle smile, 'My husband often gets frustrated with his condition. In his younger days he was always busy. If he wasn't gardening, he was fixing things. Now it's difficult for him to hold a screwdriver, much less use it.'

'All I do is sit,' Dean grumbled.

Jonas had always thought of cures with medical objectivity but, after meeting Megan's father, he wanted the researchers to have an immediate breakthrough. If anyone deserved to be hearty and whole, this man, who'd already lost a son, a daughter-in-law and his health, certainly did.

'Has your doctor talked to you about the latest treatment called DBS or deep brain stimulation?'

'He mentioned something at one time, but I've forgotten what he'd said. Back then it was experimental and I didn't pay much attention,' Nancy answered ruefully.

'In 1997, the U.S. Food and Drug Administration approved DBS for treating tremors in Parkinson's patients using a single electrode implanted in the brain. They've found that eighty per cent of the people who receive this implant show a significant suppression of their tremors. It's similar to a cardiac pacemaker.'

Dean's eyes gleamed with interest. 'What's involved?'

'As I understand it, the neurosurgeon places the tip of a hair-thin wire inside the brain in the area that controls movement. The wire then runs up through a tiny hole in the skull and under the scalp to a little device implanted under the collarbone. This device sends electrical impulses along the wire to the brain that block the faulty brain signals causing the tremor. You adjust the stimulator to match your current needs. For example, when you're stressed, you can increase the electrical impulse.'

'When he sleeps, he doesn't usually shake,' Nancy remarked. 'What happens then?'

'You turn it off, or set it on low. Because certain nerve cells become overactive and cause the muscles to be excited, hence the tremor, the idea behind this is to jam the neural network so the muscles don't react. If you'd like more information, I can suggest a few medical centers around the country where they perform the procedure, or your family doctor can refer you to the nearest facility.'

'What if it doesn't work?' Dean asked.

'I don't believe you'll be worse off than you are now,' Jonas replied, trying to recall the facts from his latest medical journal. 'They'll do some tests first to see if you'll respond before a neurosurgeon actually places the implant.'

'Pills?' Dean asked.

'For some, the DBS controls the tremors so that the levodopa and other drugs can be reduced.'

Nancy looked at her husband. 'Maybe it's time we checked into this.'

Dean nodded. 'I'd like to play with my grandchildren.'

'The internet has a lot of information and, of course, your family physician can help you locate a specialist.'

'Thank you,' Nancy said as she exchanged a glance with her husband. 'You've given us a ray of hope.'

'I'm glad.' From the interest Megan's father had shown, Jonas felt certain they would give this option due consideration.

Megan returned with a smiling Trevor on her hip and Angie trailing behind. 'We're ready,' she announced.

Angie stood on tiptoe to give her grandfather a hug and a kiss before moving on to her grandmother. Megan held Trevor while he planted a sloppy kiss on Dean's cheek, then on Nancy's.

Amid a chorus of goodbyes, Jonas helped Angie into one of the child seats they'd taken from Megan's car while Megan buckled Trevor into his. 'This vehicle isn't made for a family,' Jonas joked as he pulled away from the curb.

'Cramped, but cozy,' Megan said.

'Has your dad been in a wheelchair long?'

'He normally gets around with a walker, but when the kids are there, he doesn't want to risk tripping over them. Why?'

'Just wondering.'

Thirty minutes later, with a brand-new battery in his trunk, Jonas drove into the fast-food chain's drive-through lane. After paying for two Happy Meals, he headed for Megan's house.

'Aren't you going to eat, Mommy?' Angie asked.

'Jonas and I are going out to dinner. We have a sitter coming to his house to look after you and Trevor.'

'Do all mommies and daddies go out to dinner?'

Megan exchanged an amused glance with Jonas. 'Once in a while, they do. But don't worry. We won't be gone long. Jennifer will read you a bedtime story and give you your snack, just like I do.'

'Oh. Well, I guess that's OK. So we're staying at Jonas's house again?'

'Do you mind?' Jonas asked.

'No. We like it.'

'You do?' he asked, surprised by her response. His house was sterile, compared to Megan's. The decor was drab and, other than a television, he had nothing to interest a small child.

'Yeah. You have a dog. I watched her from the window this morning.'

'You did? What was she doing?' Megan asked.

'Scratching. I think she needs a bath,' Angie said importantly. 'When I get dirty, I itch, so I bet she does, too.'

Jonas suspected that fleas were the true culprit. Fortunately, Angie took that moment to dig her toy out of her fast-food sack and started showing it to Trevor.

While the two were occupied, Megan leaned closer. 'You realize that Angie will probably remind you in the morning to give your dog a bath.'

'I was hoping she'd forget,' he confessed.

She grinned. 'She won't. Kids have the most remarkable ability to remember the things you don't want them to.'

He groaned. 'I don't know the first thing about bathing a dog.'

'Then we're even. It can't be worse than a baby, though.'

'You don't need to worry about young Trev taking off down the street at a gallop,' he said in droll tones.

She giggled and the sound was music to his ears. 'Not yet, anyway. Look at the bright side. She'll be presentable for a family.'

'A professional groomer would do a much better job.'

'Probably, but think of the fun you'll miss.'

'Yeah, soaked from head to tow and smelling of dog dip.' He shook his head. 'I'll pass.'

He pulled into her driveway and his thoughts turned to other things besides his dog. 'I'll take care of your car while you three go in and do whatever you need to do.'

'Thanks for everything. You don't know how much I appreciate it.'

He grinned. 'Glad to be of service. See you in a few hours.'

Reassured by Jonas's insistence that replacing the battery was a one-man job, Megan hurried into the house with the children. She had a few hours to feed both, give evening baths, pack their clothes for tomorrow and a few toys for tonight, and make herself presentable for the ritziest restaurant in town.

She hadn't felt this excited since her high school prom.

Two hours later, everything and everyone was in order, except her. Clad in her old terrycloth bathrobe, she stood in front of her closet and pondered her choices. What should she wear? Nothing seemed appropriate.

The denim skirt wasn't dressy enough. The red sequined party dress was overkill. Her dark green halter dress seemed far too provocative, all things considered, but her cowl-necked sweater dress seemed too old-maidish.

Angie bounced on her bed. 'The shirt with the beads is pretty.'

'It is, isn't it?' Megan mused aloud as she pulled the hanger off the rod and surveyed the short-sleeved, cream-colored top. The faux pearls and sequins had turned a plain garment into a dressy creation. If she teamed it with a navy skirt, it might do, she decided as she slipped the shirt over her head and stepped into her skirt. Perfect, she thought as she studied her reflection. Elegant, but not ostentatious. With a pearl choker and matching earrings, she was set.

Angie and Trevor watched in fascination as she applied her make-up. Was a touch of perfume too much? Before she could talk herself out of it, she applied a few drops to her wrists and behind her ears, then declared herself ready.

'You're so pretty, Mommy,' Angie crooned.

Trevor babbled nonsense, as if he agreed.

Megan smiled at the two on her bed. 'Thanks, guys. Let's get our coats and we're off.'

She glanced at herself one final time in the full-length mirror. The reflection showed a calm, self-possessed woman, quite unlike the real one who'd developed a sudden case of stomach butterflies.

Don't read more into this evening than it is, she reminded the girl in the mirror. She wasn't looking for a relationship and neither was Jonas. They were simply going to enjoy each other's company and she'd do well to remember it.

Jonas followed Megan to their table for two and quickly hid the sappy grin that threatened to spread across his face. Ever since Megan had appeared in his doorway, he'd been completely dazzled. He'd always thought her beautiful but, dressed as she was, tonight he could only describe her as gorgeous.

And for tonight she was his. His only regret was that West Ridge didn't offer dancing like some of the other country clubs he'd frequented. He would have liked to have held her in his arms and slowly swayed to the music. Maybe next time, he thought.

'This is quite a place,' she said after they'd ordered filet mignon and twice-baked potatoes.

He'd eaten in far more elaborate surroundings, but for a

town this size the West Ridge Country Club was impressive. The furnishings and woodwork were of polished oak and the fixtures were brass that shone under the chandeliers.

'It is nice,' he said. 'So you've never been here before?'

'Dwight…' She paused, as if mentioning his name had somehow dimmed the glowing atmosphere. 'Dwight has come once or twice, but I've never been inside. Until now.'

Jonas chalked another point in Dwight's debit column with glee. How could he not have brought Megan at least once?

'How do you feel about him now?' he asked. Perhaps he was pressing on an old wound, but Dwight would be in town long after he himself had gone. Ignoring his existence would be impossible and oddly enough, Jonas wanted some reassurance that Megan wouldn't go back to him in a moment of weakness.

'No. As far as I'm concerned, he's simply one more physician who occasionally comes to the ER when we need his specific abilities. Whatever we had is over.'

Her vehemence soothed his masculine ego. He'd hoped that a woman who could set his body on fire with a simple touch wouldn't carry a torch for such an unworthy guy, and his wishes had come true. Megan deserved a fellow who thought the sun rose and set in her.

'The children need someone who loves them as much as I do,' she continued. 'If anything happens to me, I want to be sure they'll be taken care of properly.'

He thought back to his own childhood. His father had made similar plans for such an eventuality, although, without any family to call upon, he'd usually listed one of his buddies at his current posting. His dad had never said, but Jonas suspected that the older he became, the harder it had been to find someone willing to take on a teenager.

'My dad did the same thing,' he said. 'Otherwise I don't know where I would have gone after he was killed.'

'What happened?'

Jonas minimized the details. 'He went on a training mission and his plane crashed due to a mechanical difficulty. Of course, whenever he had a mission, I moved in with a different family for the duration. I wanted to stay at home, but his superiors didn't look too kindly on a teenager living alone, even if it was only for a few weeks. Anyway, this time he didn't come back and I had to stay with the Gardners.'

'How old were you?'

'Seventeen. About the time I graduated from high school, Bill—that is, Staff Sergeant Gardner—received his transfer papers. Fortunately, my dad's benefits made it possible for me to go to college so I struck out on my own.'

'It must have been tough.'

'Other than missing my dad, it wasn't. Not really.' At her incredulous expression, he tried to explain. 'With all the families I lived with over the years, I'd learned not to grow too attached to them because I knew that eventually we'd go our separate ways. As for living by myself, I had the same chores, did the same laundry, although I didn't have anyone to take a turn at the stove.' He grinned.

'So you *can* cook?' she asked.

She'd obviously noticed his bare cupboards. 'Yeah, I can, but I usually don't unless the mood strikes. Enough about me. Tell me something I don't know about Megan Erickson.'

She chuckled. 'There isn't much to tell. My brother, John, and I had an uneventful childhood. We grew up in Stanton and I went to nursing school in Omaha while he studied computer programming. I worked there for several years until Dad was diagnosed with Parkinson's.'

'So you moved back.'

'It seemed the right thing to do. The hospital advertised

for an ER nursing position at the same time, so it was fated.'

'And what do you do in your spare time?'

She laughed. 'Spare time? What's that?'

He grinned. 'Point taken. I'll rephrase my question. What did you do when you *had* spare time?'

'My friend Serena and I are members of a bicycling club, although I haven't gone on any excursions since John's accident. On occasion, I golfed. Now I feel lucky if I have a few hours to read the paper. Is your cellphone on?'

'Yes,' he said, taking her abrupt change in conversation in his stride. 'Jennifer has the number. If she has any problems, she'll call.'

Even in the dim light, he could see the faint tinge of color creep across her face. 'I'm sounding over-protective, aren't I?' she asked.

'A little, but it's understandable.'

The waiter brought their food and Jonas steered the conversation to anecdotes about the places where he'd worked. After a rich dessert of cherry chocolate cheesecake and coffee, he rose. 'Shall we go?'

For an instant, disappointment flashed across her face. 'We should,' she agreed. 'Trevor and Angie—'

'Are doing just fine,' he said firmly as he guided her to a different door than the one they'd entered by. 'Did you know there's a garden outside, complete with walking paths? A few benches, too, if the stories I've heard are true.'

'Should I assume these are strategically placed benches?' she asked with a twinkle in her eye.

'I wouldn't be surprised,' he answered, intending to take advantage of any private moments that might present themselves.

He ushered her past the tuxedo-clad *maître d'* and, ignoring his broad smile, guided Megan through the glass doors onto the terrace. Pots of sweet-smelling flowers scented the air and white lights that had been wound around various bushes and tree branches sparkled in the darkness.

'This is beautiful,' she said, her voice husky. 'It seems so magical.'

Jonas took her hand and threaded her arm through his. 'Shall we see the rest?'

He set a slow pace, mainly because he wanted to prolong the experience. For a man who was never at a loss for words, talking seemed out of place. They walked in companionable silence until the path turned back in the direction from which they'd come. Megan sank onto a nearby stone bench.

'Feet hurt?' he asked, realizing that her high-heeled strappy sandals weren't the most appropriate footwear for a garden tour.

'No. I just want to sit here and soak up the ambience. Thanks for bringing me. I'll never forget this.'

He sat beside her. 'Neither will I.' Without giving himself time to reconsider, he did the only thing a man could do when he had a most attractive woman in a romantic atmosphere. He flung one arm around her and kissed her.

Megan was positive that someone had set off fireworks. Jonas's tongue touched her lips and she opened her mouth to invite him in. She tasted coffee and chocolate and knew she'd never think of those flavors in the same way again.

Her hand rested on his arm and she felt his muscles underneath his dinner jacket. He was warm and solid, a steady rock to lean on. It seemed a shame that this special night would eventually end, but she intended to enjoy every moment while it lasted.

A breeze stirred and wind chimes hanging from tree branches tinkled merrily. She shivered, as much from the cool air as from her own reaction, and he slowly broke their contact.

'Are you cold?' he asked.

'No.' If anything, she was so hot she could burst into flame. 'Do you ever wish that things could be different?'

He stroked the side of her face. 'What would you wish for?'

*For you to never leave.* Because she couldn't say that, she lightened her tone. 'To eat all the dessert I wanted and not gain an ounce. To sleep longer than five hours a night. To have my house back.'

'Your house will be better than new a week from now, and it won't be long before you'll be complaining about Trevor and Angie sleeping the day away. As for the dessert issue—' he pointedly eyed her from head to toe '—you look good to me.'

Her face warmed under his glowing appraisal. 'Thanks, but I wasn't fishing for a compliment.'

'I know. I wanted to give you one anyway.' He glanced at his watch. 'It's ten-thirty. Do you think—?'

She jumped to her feet. 'Ten-thirty? I promised Angie we'd be home at ten.'

'Don't worry. She's either in bed or has been having too much fun to notice the time.'

He was right. Both children were asleep and had been for an hour, Jennifer assured her when they arrived back at Jonas's. Later, after they'd each retreated to their separate bedrooms, Megan thought about the things Jonas had told her. She understood how a young boy who'd been bounced from place to place had learned not to become attached to anyone or anything. It was so sad, because Jonas was wasting so much of himself by flitting from place to place and person to person.

She'd like to teach him how to unlearn the hard-life lessons he'd already learned, but she wasn't sure she was the right woman for the job.

Tonight would be her last night in Jonas's house, and

after that he'd drop out of their lives as quickly and as quietly as he'd entered. It was for the best, but sometimes 'the best' was a bitter pill to swallow.

Although Megan had reservations about Jonas's suggestion to have dinner each night at his house until her kitchen was restored, she accepted his offer for the children's sake. No one seemed to mind this new arrangement, but at times she wondered if allowing him to be a part of their lives in this small way would eventually come back to haunt her. On the other hand, she enjoyed his company as much as Angie and Trevor did and didn't have the heart to end these nightly visits prematurely.

By Thursday evening her house was fully restored to its pre-fire condition. She'd expected their dinner plans to end, but Jonas hadn't said anything and she didn't want to mention it either. For the moment she was happy to let things ride, but the moment of reckoning would come.

On Friday morning he strode into the lounge where the staff had congregated for their department luncheon meeting. 'I hope none of you are hungry,' he said. 'I just heard the news over the police scanner. There's been an accident at the airport.'

The rustling of sandwich wrappers stopped immediately and Megan's breath froze in her chest.

'A bunch of people were skydiving today,' he went on to explain. 'One fellow's parachute didn't open soon enough. He had a pretty rough landing.'

Megan inwardly winced at the thought. 'Ouch.'

'It's worse than ouch,' Jonas told her. 'According to the paramedics, he has multiple fractures, including possible left lower rib and hip fractures, and who knows what else. We're going to have our work cut out for us.'

He turned to Louise. 'Alert Radiology and the lab. I want a technician from both departments here on the double, ready to take pictures and draw blood. And you'd better call in Samuels. I can almost guarantee we'll need his surgical expertise.'

The potential for organ damage caused by the blunt trauma and/or broken ribs puncturing the liver or spleen was great. It would be best to have a surgeon standing by.

'What about orthopedics?' Megan asked.

'Yeah, you'd better get Redding here, too,' he agreed.

'How much time do we have?' Megan asked.

'Five minutes. Ten, tops.'

'We'd better get ready.'

The group scattered as each person prepared for the incoming patient. Like everyone else, Megan grabbed a yellow disposable gown from the cart near the desk where a ready supply was always available and quickly donned it over her uniform. Next came the latex gloves and a clear face shield.

Although this particular injury hadn't come into her ER before, she'd seen enough car-accident victims to know that she and her staff should be ready for anything.

The ambulance arrived, delivering a man in his early thirties who appeared every bit as badly injured as Megan had imagined, and then some. He was splinted from head to toe and, as far as she could tell, there wasn't an inch on Blake Coolidge's body that wasn't damaged in some way.

'Rapid, shallow breathing,' the paramedic reported. 'Pulse rate keeps climbing and he's been restless.'

Jonas immediately focused on the first concern—the airway. 'Flail chest,' he diagnosed after a quick glance.

Megan realized their patient had broken two or more adjacent ribs in several places. The next concern was hypoxia, or lack of oxygen to the tissues, which occurred because of an underlying pulmonary contusion. The force that had caused his ribs to fracture had probably damaged his lung and caused him to bleed inside the organ itself.

'Oxygen sat. is eighty-five,' she said, reading the number from the pulse oximeter she'd affixed to the patient's right index finger.

'Get a blood gas, stat. And let's get a picture of his chest and cervical spine so we know what we're dealing with.'

Gene moved in to draw the arterial blood sample and the venous samples for the usual CBC, chemistries, coagulation studies, a blood type and cross-match. Megan stepped aside for the radiology tech and her portable unit but stayed close to watch for signs of shock.

'Did anyone notify his family?' Jonas asked.

The paramedic replied, 'The sheriff's deputy was going to locate his wife.'

Blake's treatment proceeded like a well-choreographed production. The X-rays showed the fractured rib areas and, miraculously enough, no breaks in his spinal column, but between Jonas's endotracheal airway and the one hundred per cent oxygen, Blake's breathing wasn't improving significantly.

'Blood pressure is dropping,' Megan reported. 'Pulse is fast. Skin is cool and clammy.'

'Shock,' Jonas said. Immediately he turned his attention to Blake's abdomen. From where Megan was standing, she could see it was rigid and the area appeared bruised. 'He's bleeding inside.'

The force of hitting the ground had obviously damaged more than just his lungs and his bones. He most likely had injured other organs such as the spleen and liver.

Megan knew that in cases of shock caused by blood loss, it was imperative for that loss to be replaced with saline and/or a blood product. However, a balance had to be found because too much fluid would undo their treatment of his chest condition.

Jonas snapped orders, and it took longer than Megan would have liked before Blake's condition stabilized.

'Get another hemoglobin level,' forty-five-year-old Dr Samuels ordered. 'And send him to the OR. We'll do a laparotomy and see what's going on in there.'

As expected, Blake's H and H had dropped and two surgical staff members arrived soon after to whisk him away.

'What about his broken bones?' Megan asked Jonas when all that was left of the past several hours of excitement was a trashed trauma room.

'Samuels has to take care of the internal bleeding first,' he replied. 'Fractures won't matter if he hemorrhages to death.'

'What do you suppose he broke?'

Jonas grinned boyishly, still clearly high from his adrenaline rush. It was always a thrill to keep a patient alive long enough so that someone could repair the damage, and Megan felt her own measure of pride in their team's accomplishment.

'Out of hundreds of bones, take your pick,' he answered. 'He could have damaged the biggest share of them.'

Megan sympathetically shook her head.

'From what I could see, he's going to be in a body cast for a long while. Since I'm guessing how he landed, he's probably broken his pelvis if not both hips. His legs seemed in worse shape than his arms, but I'd bet they're fractured in at least one area, too.'

'Will he walk again?'

'Right now, walking is the least of his worries. First he has to make it through surgery and the next forty-eight hours. The possibility of complications, like a fat embolism, is high.'

Megan remembered that an embolism was simply a condition where material, such as a clot, air, fat or other foreign body, was carried by the blood from point A to point B where it lodged and obstructed blood flow. Pelvic, tibial or femoral fractures carried a high risk for fatty embolisms because of the marrow now exposed to his general circulation. Blake would require round-the-clock nurses to watch for this life-threatening condition.

'Then we're talking an extensive stint in our ICU,' Jonas added, 'not to mention months as an inpatient, followed by even longer months of rehab. He may walk again, but he may not.' He shrugged. 'I wouldn't want to predict either way.'

Suddenly, something he'd once told her popped into her head. 'Didn't you used to skydive?'

'Yeah.' His eyes took on a far-away appearance as if he was reliving those times. 'There's nothing like jumping out of a plane with the wind rushing past you and the ground rising to meet you.'

She shuddered at the thought.

'Dr Taylor?' Louise appeared at the trauma-room door. 'Mrs Coolidge is in the lobby.'

He frowned. 'Didn't Samuels see her?'

Louise shook her head. 'She arrived after he left. Shall I send her to the OR waiting room?'

'I'll talk to her first.' He glanced at his watch. 'It's nearly three o'clock,' he said, sounding surprised. 'Where did the day go?'

'Time flies when you're having fun,' Megan replied, realizing that she needed to take her meds. While he disappeared to talk to Melody, Megan swallowed her pills before she started restoring the room to rights. Gene and Bonnie had both taken other, more minor cases, which left her alone to do the honors.

She was also left alone with her thoughts.

Those at the moment were more the stuff of nightmares. A mental image of Jonas jumping out of a plane formed. In her mind's eye, she saw his chute not opening, and watched him land on the ground in a heap of broken bones and bleeding body parts.

If that ever happened, she'd never be able to bear it. What was more troubling was that if such a thing occurred after he left Stanton, she'd never know about it.

Feeling helpless, she sank onto the gurney. She hadn't meant to grow fond of him, but she had. He'd sneaked into her heart and she was powerless to evict him.

The truth was, she didn't *want* to evict him. Even knowing he would one day walk away, she couldn't say goodbye before it was absolutely necessary.

*Do you love him?*

No, she told herself. She enjoyed his company and certainly had feelings for him, but it wasn't love. It *couldn't* be love. Jonas was simply a friend who was helping her heal from Dwight's rejection.

*Friends don't kiss like he does.*

She forced that thought out of her mind. They were friends, she insisted. She could let a friend go, but not someone she loved.

'Hey, are you OK?'

Jonas's concerned tone brought her back to earth. She pasted a smile on her face. 'I'm fine. Why did you ask?'

'You looked strange. How are those meds working for you?'

'My symptoms are tolerable now, but not gone by any means. I'm not complaining. By the way, have you heard if Susan has had any luck in locating Carl Walker?'

'I talked to her a little while ago. She's still working on it. Hey, do you mind if we take your mini-van to the vet's this evening?'

She grinned. 'Don't you want to get dog hair in your sports car?'

'Dog hair I can live with,' he replied. 'I just don't think I'll have room for two adults, two children and one very large dog.'

'OK. We'll pick you up at five.'

'No later,' he warned. 'The office closes at five-thirty.'

'We'll be there. You do realize it would be easier if you went by yourself.'

'It would be,' he agreed, 'but Angie would be so disappointed. She'd never forgive me.'

Megan wondered why he would care, but the fact that he did touched her. Jonas was a special man, a veritable prince, but if she didn't stop thinking of him in those terms, she would be in far worse trouble than she already was.

She saw those qualities again a few hours later after she parked in front of the vet's office and took Trevor out of his car seat. He squirmed and wailed his displeasure until Jonas came around the vehicle and took him from her arms.

In an instant the tears of rage disappeared and a happy smile stretched across his tiny features.

Megan was astounded as much by Trevor's actions as Jonas's inclination to take over as if he'd done it a thousand times before. 'I can't believe he wants you to carry him. I'm not complaining, but if I'm around, he usually wants me.'

Jonas poked a finger in Trevor's tummy, sending the youngster into gales of laughter as he scrunched his shoulders and grabbed for Jonas's hand. 'There's a first time for everything.'

At that moment a flash of blinding insight made what she'd started to suspect and refused to believe an unalterable fact.

He was so right—there *was* a first time for everything. For her, she'd truly fallen in love.

## CHAPTER EIGHT

IT COULDN'T *be,* Megan thought numbly as she watched Angie slide her small hand into Jonas's larger one. She wasn't looking for love. If she had been, she certainly wouldn't have chosen a man who lived out of a suitcase and proclaimed himself a nomad.

Yet the more she searched inside herself, the more she realized it was true. She *had* fallen in love.

Reason demanded otherwise, but in her heart her feelings for Jonas were undeniable and exceeded those she'd had for Dwight. She supposed it was only logical to fall in love with a man who made her feel as if she were the most special person in the entire world. What woman could resist a guy whose kiss turned her insides to mush and made her skin tingle as it clamored for his touch? And how could she hold out against the same man who also took a genuine interest in her children?

The question burning in her mind was what was she going to do with her newfound knowledge?

Nothing, she decided. If he knew how quickly she'd tumbled head over heels, he'd disappear in a flash. She'd already borrowed a page from his book and decided to simply enjoy their time together for however long it lasted. But now that she knew she loved him, she wanted more than precious memories for the days ahead. She wanted Jonas himself and she refused to settle for anything less. She simply had to figure out a way to help him put aside his own fears of commitment.

Jonas halted in his tracks to glance over his shoulder at her. 'Are you coming?'

She shook herself out of her mental fugue and hurried to catch up. 'Sorry. My mind wandered there for a minute. Here, I'll get the door.'

Inside the vet's office, Megan stood next to Jonas and her family at the counter as they waited for the vet assistant's attention. Although Megan held out her arms to Trevor, the toddler dug his face in Jonas's neck and hung on tightly as if to insist on staying right where he was.

'He's fine,' Jonas told her. 'I don't mind holding him.'

He seemed sincere, but Megan didn't want him to think he didn't have a choice. 'Are you sure?'

'Yeah. In case you're worried, I haven't dropped a baby yet.'

She laughed at his comment. 'I feel so much better now.'

'Mommy,' Angie asked, 'why does it smell funny in here?'

'That's the disinfectant and the floor cleaner,' she told her. The odor wasn't unlike what she smelled on a daily basis, but quite a bit stronger.

'Is our dog going to smell like this?' she asked.

'No,' Megan reassured her.

The girl wearing a blue lab coat finally finished the note she'd been writing and flashed a welcoming smile at Jonas. 'What can I help you with?' she asked.

'I brought a dog in this morning,' Jonas said. 'A golden retriever.'

'Oh, yes. She's ready to go. I'll get her.' She disappeared into the kennel area and soon returned with the animal on a leash.

'Ooh, she's so pretty,' Angie exclaimed, echoing Megan's thoughts. Now that it had been groomed, the retriever's dingy yellow coat had become the color of burnished copper.

'She cleaned up nicely,' the assistant said, clearly pleased. 'Brushing and combing her a couple of times a week will help her stay clean and neat. Retrievers shed a lot, you know.'

Jonas assumed as much and he mentally added a brush and comb to its box of doggy possessions. He was beginning to think that owning a pet was like having a kid when one considered all the paraphernalia associated with each.

Neither was it surprising that his med school buddy had given away his dog. What *did* seem amazing was why anyone bothered to *keep* one.

'Her vaccinations are all up to date now and our tests didn't detect any parasites.' She handed the leash to Jonas and he in turn passed it to Megan.

'How old is she?' he asked.

'I'll get Dr Millard and you can ask him,' the girl said. A few minutes later, she returned with the balding forty-year-old veterinarian who wore jeans and a blue tunic.

'Hi, Jonas,' he said with a broad smile.

'Doug,' Jonas acknowledged. 'How's the golf game?'

'I played Sunday,' Doug admitted, 'but I should have stayed home and watched the pros on television. How about you?'

Jonas grinned. 'My score was bad enough on Saturday that I needed a week to recover. I really appreciate you working this dog into your schedule on such short notice.'

'After I beat you by six strokes, I figure you deserved a break.'

'Thanks, but be prepared for a rematch,' Jonas joked. 'So, what can you tell me about her?' He motioned toward the dog, who patiently sat on her haunches.

'She's probably three or four and in good health—no signs of the hip or elbow dysplasia that we often see in this breed.' He bent down and scratched the retriever's ears. 'She has a sweet disposition, so I'm guessing she hasn't been abused. Retrievers do like to follow their noses and wander, but I'm not aware of anyone looking for one that matches her description. My guess is that whoever owned her changed his or her mind.'

'So they dropped her off in the country to fend for herself,' Megan finished.

Doug gave a fatalistic shrug. 'It happens. She looks like she's had a few litters, so you might want to consider bringing her back for a little surgery. Unless you want to raise puppies, too.'

Jonas' grin was rueful. 'I don't want to raise a pet of any kind, young or old.'

'Then it's something you or her new owner will need to consider. I wouldn't put off the decision too long for obvious reasons.'

'Thanks, Doug.'

'Let me know if I can help again,' he said before he disappeared into the back office.

'At least we know why she acts so calm,' Megan said. 'She's outgrown her rambunctious puppy stage.'

'Your dog hasn't acted aggressive or hyperactive, like some we get,' the assistant offered. 'Just remember, though, that golden retrievers love to go on brisk walks and run in open spaces. I took her out earlier and she loves to fetch. Frisbees work great.'

While Jonas was digesting this information and wondering when he'd exercise his unwelcome responsibility, the girl keyed a few strokes on her computer, then handed him a tag. 'All I need now is a name.'

'Jonas Taylor.'

She chuckled. 'For the dog.'

'I have no idea what her name is.' Jonas sounded surprised. 'She just walked into my yard last week and hasn't left.'

She didn't appear concerned. 'Then you have the honor of giving her one.'

'But why do you need a name?' he asked.

'We usually list the pet's name next to the owner's in our records.'

'I'm not the owner,' he protested. 'She's a stray. I only brought her here to make sure she was healthy before I gave her away. You don't know of anyone who wants a retriever, do you?'

'Not at the moment. If you'd like to put a notice on our bulletin board, you certainly can.' She pointed to the far wall where the corkboard was covered with fliers for dog grooming services, farriers, kennels and registered Persian cats.

'So, do you want to choose a name for her?'

For lack of a better word, he promptly said, 'Girl.'

Angie, who had spent the last few minutes petting a tolerant retriever, objected. 'We can't call her that. Not when she looks as bright and shiny as a new penny.' Her eyes brightened. 'Why can't we call her Penny?'

Immediately the dog woofed, as if giving her stamp of approval.

'If it wasn't her name before, she certainly likes it now,' Megan commented.

Jonas sighed, giving in to the inevitable. 'Penny it is.'

The assistant typed on the keypad. 'You really should consider putting her on heartworm medicine.'

He frowned. His benevolent gesture was turning into far more than he'd anticipated. 'I thought you said she didn't have any parasites.'

'She doesn't. The medicine is strictly preventative. Once animals get heartworms, their treatment runs into several hundred dollars. Prevention is cheaper in the long run.'

While he paused to weigh his options, Megan interrupted. 'You can send the pills with her to her new home, along with the dog food.'

Knowing he didn't have a choice, he let out a faint sigh. 'All right. Give me a few doses.'

After several more keystrokes, a receipt rolled out of the printer. The assistant pulled a small package out from under the counter and placed it on top. 'There are six chewable squares, each square to be given once a month. Try to give it on the same day each month for maximum effectiveness.'

'OK.'

'In case you decide on birth control for your pet, Dr Millard performs his elective surgeries on Fridays. We like to schedule those procedures a week ahead of time.'

Overwhelmed by all the information and instructions, Jonas simply said, 'I'll think about it.'

Jonas juggled Trevor to dig out his billfold and pay the bill. He nearly gasped at the figure, but didn't.

Megan, however, made a small, throaty sound. 'That's three times as much as I pay for Trevor's well-baby check-ups,' she mumbled in a voice for his ears only.

'And you wonder why I don't want the responsibility of a dog?' he mumbled back.

'Now that you've decided on a name, would you like a tag?' the assistant asked. 'We can engrave her name, along with your address and phone number, in case she's ever lost.'

'No, thanks,' Jonas replied firmly.

Eager to leave before the woman tried to sell him a personalized doghouse, too, Jonas snapped his fingers at Penny, said, 'Let's go, girl,' and started toward the door. It took some doing to get everyone into Megan's mini-van, but soon they were on the road.

'Have you been calling her Girl all this time?' Megan asked, curious.

'It may not be original, but it's appropriate,' he said defensively. 'I assumed the new owners would prefer to have the honor.'

'I'm glad we picked Penny,' Angie said from the back seat.

'I was thinking along the lines of Rover,' he said. 'After all, who knows how far and where she roamed before she ended in my yard?'

'Rover's a boy name,' Angie insisted. 'Penny's a girl.'

'You chose very well,' Megan assured her. 'I doubt if either of us would have thought of it.'

'I'll second that,' Jonas said wryly. This whole incident had taken on surreal qualities. His stray dog, the one who was supposed to have moved on after it had regained its strength, now had a name to go with its special dog food, heartworm chewables and a rabies tag that led directly to him.

Even now, with a sweet-smelling dog in the back seat, he couldn't believe how his kind gesture had turned into a major responsibility. Giving the dog leftovers to eat and water to drink was a far cry from being worried about birth control and heartworms, for Pete's sake!

He frowned as he planned ways to find it—*Penny*—a new home.

'Having second thoughts?' Megan asked, as if she'd read his mind.

'Second, third and fourth,' he admitted.

'You could have taken her to the Humane Society.'

'I should have. I really thought she'd leave after a few days, though.'

'She hasn't, so maybe that's a sign you should keep her.'

'I can't,' he said flatly. 'I'll be moving soon. Trying to find an apartment that allows dogs, especially one her size, won't be easy.'

'But not impossible.'

No, it wasn't, but he didn't want the hassle. Even if Penny was good company, someone to welcome him home each night, he didn't want the ties.

'I thought all men, especially bachelors, liked owning a dog.'

'Why would you think that?'

She shrugged. 'It's someone to talk to.'

'I prefer two-legged conversationalists.'

'A dog could bring your slippers to you.'

'I don't wear slippers.'

'You can train her to fetch your newspaper. You heard the lady say she liked to fetch, which stands to reason since Penny's a retriever.'

'I buy my paper at the hospital.'

'Penny would be a warm body to curl up with on cold winter nights. Someone who won't expect anything more than a scratch behind the ears, a tummy rub and a brisk walk for exercise.'

The only warm body Jonas wanted beside his was seated behind the wheel. As for scratches, tummy rubs and exercise, he'd rather share such activities with the woman in arm's reach, not a four-legged furball.

'Well, now,' he drawled. 'Not to point out the obvious, but I prefer doing those things with someone from my own species.' He grinned. 'Plus, I don't have to worry about my date shedding hair all over the furniture.'

Megan turned a bright shade of pink. 'I suppose, with a girl in every port, a dog wouldn't compare.'

Wishing that Megan would be the girl for him in this particular port, and that she wasn't the hearth-and-home type, curiosity drove him to ask, 'Does it bother you to know I've, um, dated a lot?'

'By dating, I assume you mean…'

'I'm not in the habit of playing Russian roulette with my health. On the other hand, I haven't lived a celibate existence either.' He grinned. 'I'm rather discriminating about who I sleep with.'

'Am I supposed to be impressed?'

'Reassured,' he corrected. Then, because she hadn't answered his original question, he asked again. 'Does my history bother you?'

A small smile tugged at her mouth. 'Should it?'

He'd hoped she would have said the opposite. He certainly didn't like to think about her and Dwight sharing a bed. Just a mental image of Dwight trying to kiss her made him jealous enough for his blood pressure to rise twenty points.

'As far I'm concerned,' she added airily, 'if you have to "play doctor" so often, it only means that you're still working on your technique. You know what they say, "Practice makes perfect."'

Seeing her prim expression, he laughed. 'Are you volunteering to help me with my bedside manner?'

She chuckled. 'I would, but I'm under orders to behave myself.'

'I'll have to have a talk with your physician,' he returned.

'It won't do any good.' She sighed melodramatically. 'He's a real stickler for following instructions.'

He snapped his fingers. 'Just my luck.'

'Seriously though,' she said, 'why *haven't* you settled down? Surely you've met a woman or two who was special enough to plant those thoughts in your head.'

'They were already married. I don't poach.'

'I was referring to *single* women.'

'There were a few,' he admitted.

'What happened?'

'Nothing, really. We just never progressed to that stage.'

'Why not?'

'I've seen enough failed marriages and relationships to know that I don't want to be a part of something that won't last.'

At first, Megan didn't answer. Then, staring straight

ahead, she spoke quietly. 'Nothing does. In the end, it's quality, not quantity, that matters.'

'I saw you and Megan out last night,' Gene mentioned during a slow time in the ER a week later.

Jonas downed half of his coffee. 'Really? I didn't see you.'

Gene chuckled. 'I'm not surprised. With Megan, her two kids and your dog, your attention was definitely occupied.'

Jonas grinned. Between Angie riding her trike ahead of them as her angel wings fluttered behind her, Penny either pulling him along because she wanted to run after Angie or weaving her way around their legs and tangling her leash in Trevor's stroller, it had made for an interesting evening walk.

He wouldn't have missed the experience for all the lemon meringue pie at the bakery.

'Yup,' Gene teased. 'From what I saw, you enjoyed yourself.'

'I did,' Jonas admitted.

'Bonnie's wondering why you haven't called her.'

To be honest, he hadn't thought about it. Life with the Ericksons had kept him busy. Now that Gene had mentioned seeing him with his entourage out for a walk, Jonas realized how much more satisfying his days had become since Megan, Angie and Trevor had been a part of them.

He liked coming home to Megan and her brood, noticing the delicious smells coming from the kitchen. It reminded him of the happier days of his childhood. As luck would have it, Megan had insisted on reciprocating and now they'd fallen into an easy routine of alternating dinner between their homes.

The spring weather allowed him to walk the six blocks with Penny and then return after dark. The next night, Megan would arrive with Trevor in his stroller and Angie on her trike. Afterwards, he and Penny would accompany them home.

It was a far cry from his former routine of hurrying to the golf course and grabbing a bite on the way, or sprucing up to take someone to dinner.

As for Bonnie, he simply hadn't found the time for her. It hadn't occurred to him until this minute that he didn't want to *make* the time. Perhaps he was mellowing, or just plain bored with the sameness of playing the field, but being around Megan and the kids suddenly had become more fun than he remembered ever having with the Bonnies of the world.

And he could remember some exciting experiences.

'I've been busy.'

'Then you don't mind if I introduce her to a friend of mine?'

'Be my guest.'

'Great.' Gene's face brightened, as if he'd been afraid he would create an incident. 'Have you found someone who wants your dog?'

'Not yet.'

'What about Megan?'

'Her daughter wants to own Penny something fierce. Megan isn't thrilled at the idea.'

'What am I not thrilled with?' she asked as she appeared in the doorway.

'Owning my dog,' Jonas said, drinking in the sight of her familiar face. In spite of her cheery smile, he noticed it seemed more forced. Her blood tests to check for drug toxicity were due today. Although she couldn't possibly have received the results already, the fact that the tests had to be run in the first place had probably reminded her of a situation she would prefer to not think about.

She leaned against the doorframe. 'Someday we'll get a dog.'

'No time like the present,' he said.

'*When* Angie and Trevor are old enough to take care of it.'

'If you start now, they'll get into the habit,' he coaxed.

'Sorry. As much as I love Penny, I'd want a smaller dog. One that won't eat us out of house and home.'

Jonas turned to Gene. 'Can you believe I'm already on my second bag of dog food?'

'Buy a bigger bag,' Gene replied.

Megan straightened. 'I'd love to discuss dogs with you, but your favorite patient is here.'

Jonas glanced at the clock as he set his mug on the table. 'Violet's early.'

'Violet? Who's Violet?' Gene asked.

'Mrs Spears,' Megan supplied. 'She's in three.'

Jonas walked with her. 'How's her leg?'

'Much better. I still can't believe we're sneaking her into the department to treat her.'

Jonas's boss had insisted that he do whatever he could to send Mrs Spears to one of the family practice clinics for treatment. Unfortunately, Violet had refused. So Jonas had taken matters into his own hands. Violet appeared promptly at seven-thirty each morning and six o'clock each night. Sympathetic staff whisked her into a room, treated her leg and sent her home without the admission clerk's knowledge.

'After today, we probably won't need to,' he said. Pausing outside room three's door, he asked, 'Are you OK?'

Megan gave a half-hearted shrug. 'Sure. Why wouldn't I be? I just had my blood taken by a student vampire with a dull needle and I have a headache and nausea that won't quit.'

'Did you take your pills?'

She glowered at him. 'I'm going to forget you said that. I'm swallowing so many pills that my stomach doesn't recognize anything unless it's in tablet form. To be honest, I'm not sure I can handle two more weeks like this.'

'You can do it,' he urged, aware of many health-care workers who'd stopped their post-exposure prophylaxis because of the side effects. 'After I finish here, I'll talk to Susan and we'll modify your dosage.'

'If you say so.'

Returning to the nurses' station, Megan knew she couldn't quit. She had too many people depending on her to take the risk, but the next fourteen days stretched ahead like fourteen years.

Louise held out two charts. 'Pick one,' she said.

Megan took the one closest and read the name. Anthony Goodman. 'Who's the other?'

'A woman with abdominal pain. I'll give her to Bonnie.'

Megan called Mr Goodman out of the waiting area and ushered him to room five. 'Have a seat,' she said, motioning to the bed.

'I'd rather not,' the sixty-year-old man answered. He wore a pair of jeans, a red plaid shirt and work boots, and his face bore the weathered appearance of a man who'd spent his lifetime outdoors and smoked. The fingernails on his right hand showed the discoloration common to nicotine use.

'You see,' he went on to explain, stretching his back as if he was trying to work out a kink. 'My back really hurts. It started about four hours ago.'

'Have you lifted anything heavy or pulled anything?'

'Nope,' Mr Goodman said, shaking his head. 'It started hurting right after I got up this morning. All I did after that was go to the donut shop for morning coffee with the rest of my poker buddies. Honest to gosh, I didn't lift anything heavier than my plastic cup, but I'm telling you, Nurse, I'm in pain.'

Megan jotted down her observations, then recorded his

vital signs. 'Put on this hospital gown so the doctor can examine you. We'll be back in a few minutes.' As an afterthought, she added, 'Do you need any help?'

'I can manage.'

By the time she returned, with Jonas in tow, Mr Goodman was sitting on the edge of the bed, his hands rubbing his lower back.

Megan had hardly closed the door when their patient begged for relief.

'Let's find out what's causing this first,' Jonas said.

Megan watched from a discreet distance while he pressed up and down Mr Goodman's back to check for sore muscles and tender vertebrae. Goodman's facial expression didn't change, so she guessed that wasn't the problem.

Jonas helped the man lie down and began checking out his abdomen. Megan saw Goodman wince as Jonas pressed on the lower left quadrant, but so far she couldn't begin to guess at what was wrong.

He pulled his stethoscope out of his coat pocket and began listening to the pulses in his patient's groin area. Although he listened intently, Megan watched his gaze travel down Mr Goodman's legs where she saw the sight that had captured Jonas's attention. A lacy pattern of blue covered his extremities, which suggested that his circulation was poor.

Finally, Jonas straightened and hung his stethoscope around his neck. 'We're going to run a few tests, Mr Goodman. The first one is an ultrasound, where we use sound waves to create a picture of what's happening inside you. I also want some blood tests so we can get an idea of your general health.'

'Can you give me something for my pain?'

'Not yet,' Jonas apologized. 'Until we know for sure what's wrong, a painkiller will only mask things. I promise, though, we'll hurry.'

He motioned Megan outside. 'Get someone from Radiology here, stat. I also want the lab here on the double and I want the usual, along with a type and cross-match for six units. I also want Life Flight put on standby.'

Life Flight was the air ambulance service that ferried their worst patients to Denver for treatment.

'He's that bad?' she asked.

'I suspect he has a leaking triple-A.'

She knew he meant abdominal aortic aneurysm.

'If I'm right,' he continued, 'I want the helicopter ready to take off as soon as the ultrasound is done. I'll be in two if you need me.'

Megan rushed to do his bidding. Their hospital wasn't equipped to handle vascular surgery, and whenever aneurysm cases appeared in the ER, time was of the essence.

Louise called the hospital departments while Megan dialed the helicopter service and explained the situation. Fortunately, they had one chopper free and would place it on standby to await her word before taking off for the thirty-minute flight from Denver to Stanton.

She returned to Mr Goodman's room to find the lab tech leaving and the ultrasound tech organizing herself and her equipment for the painless procedure. 'Dr Taylor will be waiting for those pictures as soon as you're done.'

'It won't be long,' the technician promised. Before she got too far, Jonas joined them.

'Slow day, huh, Doc?' Mr Goodman asked.

Jonas leaned against the counter where he could watch both the patient, the technician and the monitor screen. 'It is,' he said, although Megan knew it wasn't. He obviously didn't want to waste time if his suspicions were correct.

'I wonder who's going to win the World Series?' he asked.

Mr Goodman chuckled. 'It's too soon to predict, but my guess is the Yankees.'

'Really? I'm a Ranger fan myself.'

By the time they'd discussed the merits of every major league baseball team, the test was done. Jonas motioned to Megan to make the phone call and she knew what he'd found.

By the time she returned, he'd broken the news to his patient.

'This is serious, isn't it?' Mr Goodman asked.

'Yes, it is,' Jonas admitted. 'Your best hope is to get to a hospital where a vascular surgeon can repair the damaged artery. I've already alerted the staff in Denver and they're getting ready for you as we speak. You should be there in about an hour.'

'Really?' He seemed more interested in that fact than in his condition.

'Do you have anyone you'd like us to notify?' Megan asked. 'Your wife, children, a neighbor?'

'Never been married,' Mr Goodman answered. 'You could call my neighbor. Roy Knight. He'll need to look after my horses.'

'I'll tell him.' Megan set Louise to handle the job while she helped prepared Goodman for his helicopter ride. She started IVs so that, if anything happened, he'd have a line ready for use. The blood-bank staff brought the units of blood, specially packed in ice, to send along in case they were needed *en route*. Nursing notes, physician notes and copies of the ultrasound and lab results had to be prepared to accompany the patient.

By the time the Life Flight crew of a physician and a nurse arrived in their familiar blue jumpsuits, Anthony Goodman was ready to leave.

'How did you know it was an aneurysm?' Megan asked once they'd wheeled Mr Goodman out of the ER and the excitement had died down. 'I always thought they were tough to diagnose.'

'They are. As for knowing, I didn't suspect until I saw his legs. The next logical thing was an ultrasound or a CAT scan to confirm it.'

'And you were right.'

Jonas grinned, one of those smiles that showed he was pleased by his success, too. 'Lucky for him.'

'You have remarkable instincts,' she said.

'ER doctors develop them,' he said, 'otherwise we lose patients we shouldn't. It also helps because I've worked in a lot of different places and seen a lot of different things. Experience is still the best teacher.'

'Do you think he'll make it?'

'If the vessel doesn't blow on the way, he has a fighting chance. That's all we can give him.'

Without warning, Susan Forbes burst through the ER doors and flagged them down. Instinctively, Megan tensed, then decided she was overreacting. Susan could have come to the ER for any number of reasons. Her entire day certainly didn't revolve around Megan's problems.

'I'm so glad I caught you both,' Susan said. 'You'll never guess what happened.' In the next breath, before either of them could answer, she added, 'I found Carl Walker.'

## CHAPTER NINE

'You found Carl?' Megan said faintly.

Susan nodded. 'Yes. Can we talk in your office?' she asked Jonas.

'Sure.'

Megan could hardly hold her questions until they were around his desk. 'How did you find him? Where is he?'

'Whoa, there,' Susan said with a smile. 'Carl's girlfriend called the other day and gave me his telephone number. Apparently, she tracked him down to Florida where he went to stay with a friend of his. I left message after message and finally he phoned this afternoon.'

Megan focused on his location. 'He's in Florida?' That was half a country away.

'Not any more,' Susan announced. 'He started back last night and should arrive here tomorrow morning. I explained the situation and he promised to come here as soon as he arrives so we can recollect his blood sample. The lab knows he's coming and, under penalty of death, they will make sure nothing happens to it this time.'

'You're sure?'

'As sure as I can be. Tomorrow is Tuesday, so we'll have the results by Friday afternoon.'

Friday afternoon. Remembering what it had been like to wait for each day to pass, Megan wasn't sure that she wanted to know.

Yet she had to. Once and for all, good or bad, the cloud of uncertainty would disappear.

As if sensing her inner turmoil, Jonas clutched her hand. Megan didn't care if Susan, or anyone else for that matter, saw that he'd stepped beyond the boundaries of hospital colleagues. Right now, she needed his strength.

'The anticipation has been tough,' Susan said kindly. 'I don't think I need to warn you that those results could go either way.'

Megan drew a shaky breath. 'Believe me, I know.'

'You need to think about what you'll do if his Western blot results are positive.'

'I have.' The question had hovered in the back of her mind for the past two weeks. Most of the time Jonas had helped her ignore it and pretend the situation wasn't happening, but the worry had never completely disappeared.

Susan smiled. 'I don't think I need to ask what you'll do if his results are negative.'

'Other than flush the rest of my pills down the toilet?' Megan shook her head. 'No, you don't.'

Susan rose. 'I'd thought about waiting until Friday to talk to you, in case we develop another hitch in our plans, but it didn't seem right to spring this on you at the last minute.'

'I appreciate it,' Megan said.

Susan glanced at their entwined hands, but didn't comment. 'I'd like to suggest that you plan something to do on Friday, after we meet again.'

'Plan something?' Megan asked dumbly.

'An outing,' she explained. 'An event to focus on and anticipate.'

An outing. 'OK,' Megan agreed, although her mind went blank before she could think of an activity.

'Whatever you choose to do,' Susan said firmly, 'stick to it, no matter what happens or how the tests turn out.'

*No matter what.* Megan nodded.

'Then I'll see you both on Friday.'

Megan hardly noticed Susan's departure until Jonas spoke her name. 'Are you all right?'

'Yeah, sure. I think so.' Her calm suddenly deserted her

as the latest events finally soaked into her brain. 'Oh, Jonas. I want to know, but at the same time I don't.'

Everything she'd suppressed poured out and she couldn't stop the flood. 'I've tried not to ask myself what if, but I have. What if I seroconvert to positive? What kind of life will I have if I need to take these dratted pills for years on end? What if my insurance company finds out? Will they cancel my medical insurance, my life-insurance policy? Who will look after the kids? What kind of burden will I become to my friends, my family? What if…?'

She couldn't continue. It was as if the Grim Reaper had poised himself once again to strike. The stress of waiting had turned her into a near basket case last time. The prospect of going through that again brought tears.

'Shh,' he said as he pulled her to her feet. She went into his arms, and gratefully leaned on him. 'You're going to be fine.'

'What if I'm not?' she hiccuped.

'What if you are?' He wiped the moisture off her cheeks with his thumbs. 'You'll have wasted all this water for nothing.'

'But—'

'But we'll take each day as it comes,' he said firmly. 'Fill your head with ideas on what we should do Friday evening.'

She sniffled as she nodded.

'It has to be something special,' he continued. 'Something momentous.' He tipped up her chin so that her gaze met his. 'I know what I'd like to do.'

Megan dabbed her eyes. 'What?'

Hunger appeared in his eyes, as well as a decidedly feral grin. 'I think we should find a babysitter. Preferably one who can stay until the wee, wee hours of the morning.'

A fresh lake of tears brimmed in her eyes. 'You're so sweet to suggest it,' she said. 'But it can't happen.'

'Why not?'

'I won't put you at risk.' She loved him far too much to do such a thing, even though she wanted it more than she had ever imagined. 'I couldn't. I wouldn't.'

He cupped her face with his hands. 'Then we have one more reason to hope and pray the test will turn out negative.'

With that, he kissed her.

For the rest of the week, Megan pretended a calm that didn't exist as she threw herself into her routine. She doubted if anyone other than Jonas noticed her edginess, but he was partly to blame. His list of suggestions for Friday evening grew until she had more choices than she could consider. She suspected he'd done so on purpose because weighing her options didn't give her time to think about the future past Friday.

'What is something you've always wanted to do?' he'd asked. 'The Denver Symphony is performing. Or we could fly to Seattle and visit the Space Needle. Then there's a trip to Dallas so you can shop till you drop at a Nieman-Marcus store.'

'Don't be ridiculous,' she'd told him. 'I can't afford those kinds of trips, especially not on short notice.'

'Ah, but I can,' he said.

'You're independently wealthy, too?'

'I've put aside a few pennies for a rainy day. I don't live a totally dissolute life.' He winked. 'So what'll it be?'

'None of the above. I want a special evening with Trevor and Angie. We'll go to the zoo.'

His smile was benevolent. 'A trip to the zoo requires a full afternoon, if not longer. If I leave promptly at six, we'll only have an hour or two of daylight. Let's save that excursion for Saturday. Shoot, let's think bigger than Friday night and plan an entire weekend.'

'Won't you miss out on golf or the car races, or whatever else you do on your days off?'

'This is *your* weekend, not mine,' he reminded her. 'And speaking of which, I know how important Trevor and Angie are to you, but surely there's something you'd like to do just for yourself.'

*Strolling down a moonlit beach with Jonas at her side. Watching the sun set and then, after hours and hours of exploring each other until every one of her senses had reached overload, watching the sun rise and doing it all over again.*

Because ocean beaches were in short supply in Nebraska and her health too uncertain, she modified her wish slightly.

'I'd like to attend the outdoor community concert,' she said slowly. 'Just the two of us, so I can soak up the music without worrying if Angie's tired or Trevor's fussy. Then I want to sit on Painter's Point and watch the stars come out while I sip champagne and nibble on Brie and strawberries.'

'Sounds reasonable. Anything else?'

'Isn't that enough?'

'It depends,' he drawled, 'but for starters, it'll do. And just to be sure you won't change your mind, I'll handle the details, including the babysitter.'

'It won't be easy finding one,' she warned.

'Leave it to me.'

So she did. True to his word, he arranged everything, even paying Doug Millard's daughter, Jennifer, top dollar to watch Trevor and Angie.

As the days passed, her fear began to build like stormclouds on the western horizon. She envisioned every moment of her upcoming evening from the time Jonas arrived at her house to the appearance of the last star. She imagined going to his place afterward for a nightcap and staying for a special sunrise breakfast.

When Friday came, she'd expected it to drag interminably, but she'd never been busier at the hospital. Everything from dog to spider bites, a prisoner who'd swallowed a bed spring to shorten his jail time, a heart attack, bleeding ulcer and a motorcycle accident came through the double doors.

It wasn't until Susan appeared on the unit at the end of Megan's shift that she realized how swiftly the time had flown. Unfortunately, Jonas was with the motorcycle victim's wife and Megan didn't have any idea how long their visit would take.

Susan glanced at her watch. 'I'd love to wait for him, but I have another appointment. Shall we do this Monday?'

'No!' Megan lowered her voice. 'No. Tell me now. If I have to wait two more days, I'll need Valium.'

Susan smiled. 'I understand.' She pulled an envelope out of her pocket. 'I normally don't give out hard copies, but I'm making an exception in your case because I doubt if you'll believe it otherwise.'

A knot grew in Megan's throat and she struggled to swallow.

'I've blocked out the patient's identification, so you'll only see the results.'

Megan took the envelope and slid the small sheet of paper free. Hardly breathing, she unfolded it and scanned the printed page.

Her vision swam as she struggled to read the results. 'Oh, my.' She glanced at Susan. 'Oh, my.'

'I said the same thing.' Susan peered at her as she placed a hand on Megan's arm. 'You're not going to pass out, are you? Would you like a glass of water?'

Megan slid the form back into the envelope with shaky fingers and drew a deep breath—the first deep breath she felt she'd taken since her ordeal had begun. 'No. It's taking me a little time to get used to the idea that I just got my life back.'

Susan chuckled. 'I understand. I know this is a silly question, but what are you doing to do this evening?'

Megan grinned. 'What else? Celebrate.'

Jonas nearly ran down the ER hallway in his rush to find Megan. Her shift had ended twenty minutes ago and he was afraid that Susan had come and gone.

He stopped in front of the nurses' station. 'Where's Megan?' he barked at Karen, the clerk who'd taken over Louise's duties for this shift.

'She left.'

He ran his hands over his short hair. 'Do you know if she talked to Susan Forbes?'

'I think so.'

'And?'

'And what? They talked. That's all I can tell you.' She frowned at him. 'What's going on?'

'Nothing. Did Megan say anything before she left?'

'Yeah. She gave me a message for you.'

He waited expectantly. 'And?' Did he have to drag every little word out of people today?

'She said to tell you there's a change in plans.'

He raised his voice. 'A change in plans?'

'That's what she said.'

Too upset to stand still, he started to pace. 'Did she say anything else?'

Karen paused from her task of sorting files. 'Yeah, but I can't remember for sure. Something about...' Her voice died.

He stopped in his tracks and forcibly lowered his tone. 'I don't mean to be rude, but can you, please, just *spit it out*?'

Karen sniffed, clearly used to high-strung physicians.

'Well, aren't we in a bad mood? If you're in such an all fired hurry, ask her yourself.'

'She's gone,' he reminded her.

Karen waved to a spot over his shoulder. 'I was wrong. If you hurry, you can catch her.'

Jonas swirled to see the back of Megan's head as she passed through the exit. Not caring what his colleagues thought, he dashed after her and burst through the glass door as he called her name.

She stopped on the sidewalk and turned, and the tears on her face sent his heart sinking like a block of cement. Hurrying to meet her halfway, he sidestepped the foot traffic and held out his arms.

'Oh, Jonas,' she cried, as she flew into his outstretched arms.

He hugged her close, wishing he could turn the clock back to the morning before Carl Walker had come into the ER. 'It's OK,' he murmured in her ear as he stroked her soft hair.

'Oh, Jonas.' Her voice sounded choked, but there was a note he couldn't quite describe. 'I can't believe it. It doesn't seem possible.'

'Then you talked to Susan.' He stated the obvious.

'Oh, yes. I decided that I couldn't wait. She gave me the results and then we talked for a while, but you never did come back. How's the motorcycle guy?'

She'd just heard bad news and was worried about someone else? 'He's fine. What did Susan say? Was the test positive?'

Megan dug in her purse with one hand while she swiped her cheeks with the other. 'Here. I'll let you read it for yourself.'

'Tell me,' he demanded.

She stared at him, incredulous. 'I thought I did.'

'No,' he said patiently, as if talking to a child. 'You didn't.'

She grinned. 'He's negative.'

'Negative?'

She nodded as she handed over the paper Susan had given her. 'Everything was negative, including his repeat HIV screen. Susan can't explain it, except he must have had some interfering substance in his sample when the lab tested it the first time.'

Unable to contain himself, Jonas picked her up and swung her around. She squealed with delight. 'Put me down, Jonas. People are watching.'

'Who cares?' he said, although he slowly let her feet touch the concrete. He'd been fretting over the idea of leaving town without a solid support system for her in place, and now he could rest easy.

'You scared me to death,' he scolded her good-naturedly.

'When?'

'When I saw you crying.'

'Those were tears of joy.'

He knew exactly what she meant because he wouldn't have minded shedding a few himself.

'Would you mind if we changed our plans this evening?' Megan asked as Jonas parked on the street in front of the town's bandstand.

Jonas turned off the ignition key, realizing he'd forgotten that part of Karen's message in all the excitement. 'I thought the rule was that we were supposed to stick to our plan, no matter what.'

'I know. It's just that…' Her voice faded as she stared up at him.

'It's just what?'

'I feel so *antsy*, like I'm about to jump out of my skin.'

'The weatherman predicted a storm. You're probably feeling all that electricity building up.'

'What I feel doesn't have anything to do with a storm. I'm so happy, I want to just *explode* with it.'

Jonas grinned. 'A concert is a little too tame for you?'

'Crazy, isn't it?' she said. 'I've decided that I don't want to be a spectator tonight. I want something *physical*, for lack of a better word.'

He had his own ideas of physical activity, but this was *her* night and unless it was *her* suggestion, he'd keep his thoughts to himself.

'It's not crazy. You bottled up so much emotion and now it wants to come out.' He clenched the steering-wheel with a white-knuckled grip. 'What did you have in mind?'

'Tennis?'

'No racquets.'

'Jogging?'

He pointedly glanced at her clothes. She was wearing a thigh-length skirt and short-sleeved blue sweater while he'd donned a pair of tan chinos and a green plaid cotton shirt. 'We're not dressed for it.'

'Golf.'

He pointed to the horizon. 'It'll be dark soon. Why don't we hit a bucket of balls at the driving range?'

Her face brightened. 'Great. I haven't played for so long, I can use the practice.'

After she sliced and hooked her way through half a bucket, Jonas could tell she hadn't been stretching the truth.

'I give up,' she said, holding out the three-wood club she'd borrowed.

'You can't. Not yet.' Jonas put his arms around her and helped her with a few practice swings. 'Keep your head down,' he instructed, hardly able to think straight with her scent teasing his nose.

He positioned a ball in front of them and swung. 'Like that,' he said.

She tried it on her own and hooked it toward the groundskeeper.

'Fore!' Jonas yelled seconds before the man ducked and saved himself a headache.

'Oh, my gosh.' Megan covered her mouth with her hands. 'Maybe I should quit before we have to call for an ambulance.'

'You're doing fine,' Jonas said. 'Let's try again.' He gripped her hands in his as he went through the motion of swinging again. Having her nestled against him as he worked on her form and technique was like torture. After ten minutes, sweat broke out on his forehead and he wondered how he'd continue.

She turned her head so that her breath kissed his cheek. 'Maybe we should leave.'

'Leave? Now?' He didn't know if he was glad or disappointed.

'I'd like to go home.'

'Home?' He was starting to sound like a parrot. 'You want to go home so soon?'

She twisted in his arms to face him. '*Your* home. Not mine.'

Jonas couldn't believe what he was hearing and he mentally shook himself out of his dream.

'Your house,' she said softly. 'Remember how you told me that I should do something for me?'

Did he remember? His imagination hadn't stopped running since. 'Yeah.'

'Well, this is it. This is the something I want to do for me. And you,' she tacked on. 'If you want, that is.'

'Oh, I want. I definitely want.' He grabbed the club she'd been using and returned the half-empty bucket of golf balls to the clubhouse.

During the fifteen-minute drive to his place, he let Megan fiddle with the radio station settings until a romantic soft-rock song drifted out of the speakers.

She pointed in the distance as a thin flash of lightning skewered the sky. 'It looks like rain.'

'What did I tell you?' He parked in his driveway and ushered her inside. 'Let me check on Penny. She usually goes nuts when I come home.'

He didn't need to check on Penny—he knew she'd be content unless he opened the door to the backyard. He simply needed a few minutes to compose himself and to think this through. Whatever happened in the next few minutes, the next few *hours*, would completely change the tone of his relationship with Megan.

As he'd suspected before he peered through the glass, Penny was lying on the blanket he'd provided, her eyes closed.

'Is she OK?'

He turned to discover Megan standing a few steps away. 'Are you sure about this?' he asked.

'Yes.'

'Don't expect anything permanent,' he cautioned.

'I won't.'

'Would you like a glass of champagne?'

She smiled. 'Later.'

'What about…?'

Megan stepped forward. 'You're talking way too much.'

'I am, aren't I?' he said as he drew her close.

She freed the top two buttons of his shirt. 'Need I remind you that this is *my* evening?'

'No.'

'And as hard as it is to find a sitter, this could well be our only chance to be together for a while.'

He didn't need further urging. He whipped off his shirt, then hers. 'Are you ready for action?'

She stood on tiptoe to reach his mouth as he flicked the catch on her bra strap. 'Ready, willing and able.'

Megan had never realized two bodies could generate such heat. Everything about Jonas whirled around her until she couldn't tell where she ended and he began. His scent, the mint on his breath and his touch rolled over her like ocean waves, wrapping her in his essence.

Her legs moved, although she didn't understand why or where they were taking her until she felt as if gravity had disappeared and she was lying on something soft. His bed, the analytical portion of her brain identified.

Zippers rasped and more clothes disappeared as if by magic. A heartbeat later, nothing, not even air, separated them.

She ran her hands along his body, noticing the play of muscles in his arms and shoulders as he paid her equal homage. His skin was rough and the wiry hair tickled her skin as he slid over her.

'Are you sure?' He sounded hoarse as he whispered his question against her mouth.

'More than anything,' she mumbled.

She'd never dreamed how high she could soar with Jonas as a part of her. Her body trembled as she left the world behind on a flight that seemed to last for hours before she fell to earth in his arms.

Slowly he pulled away but she grunted her protest and he didn't go far. He simply tucked her against him and let the afterglow continue its soothing warmth.

Words seemed trite, so she simply let the night air wash over them. The darkness was cozy, but an occasional flash of lightning reminded her of the powerful forces they'd unleashed in this very room.

'Thank you,' she said when she could speak again.

'I should be thanking you,' he said. 'That was fantastic.'

'What can I say? We're a great team.'

As soon as she'd said it, a tremendous sense of loss came over her. They might be a great team but, no matter how much she wanted it to be otherwise, Jonas didn't form partnerships that lasted. If only knowledge could override emotions.

Megan knew nothing would come from this evening but, as she'd told him, she'd wanted this for herself. He would leave, but before then she'd enjoy what moments she could.

After this particular moment, though, she didn't understand how Jonas could walk away as easily as he did. His life could be much more full if he let himself stop wandering. If she wasn't able to convince him, she'd let him go, but she couldn't imagine falling in love with anyone else.

Then, because she wanted to keep the mood light, she asked, 'Should we break out the champagne?'

'I thought you wanted to go to Painter's Point?'

She stroked his chest. 'We could, but I think our storm will hit before we can get there.'

'It already has,' he said before he trailed kisses down her neck. 'And if I have anything to say about it, it's going to last for hours and hours.'

## CHAPTER TEN

ALONE at two a.m., but not by choice, Jonas should have been asleep, but Megan's scent had permeated his bedroom to the point where he couldn't close his eyes without imagining her beside him.

It had been an evening he would never forget, even if he lived to be a hundred and ten. Being with Megan had given him such a sense of belonging, a sense of connection that he'd never felt so strongly in his entire life.

His interlude with Megan wasn't supposed to have been like that. Sure, he'd expected to enjoy himself, to give pleasure as well as take it, but he hadn't dreamed that the experience would make all others pale in comparison.

Everything about this was so right. No one else had ever made him feel as if he was the other half of a whole. From the moment she'd undone his shirt buttons to the time when they'd sipped champagne on his bed, he'd felt as if they were two wheels with perfectly matched cogs holding them in place.

It hadn't struck him what a huge mistake he'd made until he'd taken her home at midnight. Megan wasn't one of his usual women who understood and accepted a short-lived relationship. She might *say* that she was agreeable to his here-today-gone-tomorrow approach to life, but he knew that deep down she wasn't.

She was a woman with responsibilities, a woman who wanted family ties to form a wholesome environment for Trevor and Angie. And for a short time in that room, he'd discovered a part of himself that wanted to drop on his knees and beg her to let him share her life for the next fifty or so years.

Sadly, he couldn't do it. He'd grown so used to packing up and starting over that he couldn't imagine being rooted in one place, with one person. Living without attachments was as much a part of him as his eyes.

Megan, on the other hand, needed permanence. She needed family, a spouse to help her raise the little ones, and Jonas didn't have the foggiest idea of how to be a husband, much less a parent.

Now, when he should be replaying every instant of the best night of his entire life, he was sitting on his patio deckchair, gazing into the star-studded sky and talking to his dog.

'I'm in trouble, Penny,' he said as he massaged her head. 'Megan and the kids need more than I can give them.'

Penny yawned.

'It's my own fault. I took one look at Megan and threw all my rules out the window. If I'd followed them, like I usually do, I wouldn't be in this fix.'

Penny sighed.

'I should walk away, but I can't. I know I'm being selfish, but I like the way they make me feel and I want to enjoy it for as long as I can. Is it wrong to pretend to be a part of them for two more months?'

Penny put her head on her paws and stared at him. He rubbed the scruff of her neck.

'Too bad you can't answer me,' he said. 'I could use some advice. Megan was right. You are a good listener. I just wish I knew what to do with you.'

One thing was for certain. Leaving Stanton wouldn't be easy because this time he would leave a portion of himself behind.

\* \* \*

'I hear you've been spending a lot of time with Dr Taylor,' Bonnie said a week later.

Wary, Megan studied her colleague for traces of rancor, but to her relief didn't find any. 'We've been together, yes.'

'You know that I don't care who dates who. I mean, I was a little jealous of you at first but, then, who wouldn't be? Handsome dudes with great personalities don't fall in our laps too often, if you know what I mean.'

'I think so.'

'Anyway, I'm not trying to warn you off him, but save yourself some heartache. He's not going to stick around.'

The other woman's concern touched Megan. She wouldn't have expected Bonnie to be worried about her. 'I know.'

'You do?'

Clearly she hadn't given the answer that Bonnie had anticipated. 'As much as I'd wish it were otherwise, I'm well aware that Jonas is only passing through town.'

Bonnie nodded as she studied her closely. 'I must say, you've surprised me.'

Megan grinned. 'Really? Join the club. Sometimes I surprise myself.'

'I'm serious. Here you were—engaged to Dr Fleming, with two kids—ready to step into a role that suits you perfectly, and now look at you.'

'Things change. We have to go with the flow.'

'Don't I know it. I just never would have dreamed that you'd "flow" in the direction of Dr Taylor.' She grew thoughtful. 'Although I suppose if I'd been in your shoes, a guy like Dr Taylor would be a good prescription to get me back in the dating game.'

If that was how people looked at her relationship with Jonas, then she wouldn't contradict them. However, Megan knew that no one would ever measure up to Jonas Taylor.

'Have you planned anything for the weekend?' Bonnie asked.

'We're taking the kids to the zoo. We were going to go last Saturday, but when it rained, we postponed.'

'Have a good time. I once dated a guy who worked at the zoo. He was a real tiger, if you know what I mean.' She winked.

'You are being careful, aren't you?' Megan asked, deciding to pass along a few warnings of her own. 'Safe sex and all that.'

Bonnie patted her arm. 'Don't worry about me,' she said cheerfully. 'I'm as protected as the gold at Fort Knox.'

Megan hoped so.

The ambulance bay doors whooshed open and Gene approached them at a run.

'What's up?' Megan asked as she accompanied him to the door.

'Violet Spears. Apparently she was involved in a hit-and-run.'

'After all that hard work we did on her, she ends up back here.' Megan grabbed a yellow protective gown from a cart near the door and slipped it over her clothes. 'The irony of it all.'

Jonas joined them. 'Yeah, but this time we won't have to sneak around to treat her.'

Two paramedics burst in with the gurney between them. Violet's frail body was fixed to a backboard and trails of blood ran down the left side of her face. Mud caked her entire body.

Immediately they rattled off her vital signs and listed her injuries as the group wheeled her into the nearest trauma room.

'Shattered femur from where the car struck her,' the one reported. 'Dislocated shoulder, with head and neck trauma from hitting the ground after she flew off her bicycle.'

'Where did she land?' Jonas asked. 'Pavement, concrete, what?'

'Actually, she sailed into some guy's yard, and he'd just watered his lawn so the ground was pretty spongy.'

'Let's hope it was soft enough.'

Brain injuries were tough to deal with. Their small facility simply wasn't equipped to handle such serious cases.

While Megan and Bonnie hurried to hook her up to their monitors so the paramedics could take theirs with them, Jonas fired orders for another IV, blood work, CT scans and drugs that would keep her from having seizures.

'Did she ever regain consciousness?' he asked.

'No.'

'Shall I notify Life Flight?' Megan asked.

Jonas nodded.

An hour later, the diagnosis was evident. Violet Spears had suffered a subdural hematoma, and thirty minutes after that she was on her way to a neurosurgery unit.

'What a shame,' Megan said to Jonas once all the hubbub had died down. 'She seemed like a sweet lady for all of her eccentricities.'

'She was.'

He seemed maudlin. 'Don't you think she's going to make it?' she asked.

'Who knows? She's a tough old bird so if anyone can pull through, she can. Sometimes, though, I wonder...'

He didn't finish his sentence and Megan wanted to hear what weighed on his mind. 'You wonder what?'

'I wonder if we should have let her go.' He glanced at her. 'She had no family, no friends to speak of. She is a lonely old lady who lost her husband in the Vietnam War and didn't have any children.'

'People would help her if she'd let them.'

'Maybe. Violet was—is—a proud woman. She doesn't like charity. She told me once that she was ready to go.'

'If she hadn't come in for treatment of her cellulitis, she may well have. If that's how she felt, I wonder why she bothered coming back twice a day for more than a week?'

The answer hit her. 'She came because of you, didn't she?'

His mouth twitched into a slight grin. 'I think so. She said I was the only one who cared enough to give her choices. Everyone else wanted to shuffle her off to someone else. It didn't hurt that I let her talk about her husband and her hobbies. Did you know that at one time she was a florist?'

'No, I didn't. It's no wonder it always took you so long with her,' she exclaimed. 'And here I thought you were just slow.'

'Slow!' he cried in mock horror. 'I'll have you know I won first prize in our who-can-bandage-the-fastest contest in med school.'

'You had a contest?'

'It was all part of our annual end-of-year party. I can't remember all the categories, but we had competitions for making the tightest bed corners, reassembling the anatomy professor's skeleton and gurney races. I held the record for taking the most first prizes in making the bed, too.'

She giggled. 'Making it, or messing it up?'

He wiggled his eyebrows. 'One was judged, the other wasn't. By the way, have you told Angie about tomorrow?'

'Not yet,' she admitted. 'If she knew we planned to go to the zoo, she wouldn't have given me a minute's peace. I'll tell her this evening.'

As Megan had predicted, Angie was so excited about their trip it was difficult for her to go to sleep. Megan wasn't sure if it was the excursion itself or the fact that Jonas would be accompanying them. Regardless of her reasons, Angie was thrilled and Megan mentioned it to her mother when she called at ten o'clock.

'You can't blame her for being over the moon,' Nancy said. 'Angie hasn't had this much male attention since her father died. Dwight didn't step into his role and although your father would give anything to be healthy enough so that he could, he can't. It isn't any wonder that Angie likes Jonas.'

'I know, Mom, but how will they survive when Jonas leaves?'

'Are you certain he will?'

'Absolutely. He mentioned it the other night.' She'd hoped that he would see what he was missing with each evening he spent in their company, but he obviously hadn't.

'Have you told him how you feel?'

She thought of their special night a week ago. They hadn't done a lot of talking. 'Not in so many words.'

'Maybe you should.'

Megan wasn't sure. Announcing that she loved him could backfire far more easily than it would help her cause. Then again, what did she have to lose? Either way, he'd be gone. At least he'd know exactly what he was walking away from.

But maybe she *didn't* want him to know. Her experience with Dwight hadn't boosted her ego to the level of being able to weather another rejection.

'As for the children,' Nancy continued, 'Trevor won't remember, but if Angie doesn't hold false expectations, then she'll cope, just as you will.'

Megan hoped her mother was right.

'What's first, the birds or the monkeys?' Jonas asked Angie as they approached the zoo entrance.

'The monkeys,' Angie exclaimed, clutching her hat on her head with one hand while she adjusted her blue plastic sunglasses with the other.

'The monkey section it is,' Jonas said as he pushed Trevor's stroller through the open wrought-iron gates.

Too excited to walk beside them, Angie ran ahead. 'Stay where we can see you,' he cautioned.

'OK.'

Jonas leaned closer to Megan. 'I'm surprised she didn't wear her wings.'

'I am, too, but I've noticed that lately she hasn't been wearing them as often. They were her security blanket in some respects, and I think she's finally adjusting to the changes in her life.'

'I'm glad.'

The bird exhibit was next and because it was one where the visitors could walk through the animals' natural habitat and see them close up, Angie held onto Megan's hand while Jonas carried Trevor.

They walked for what Jonas thought was equivalent to thirty-six holes of golf, but he didn't mind. It was a treat, seeing everything through Angie's innocent eyes.

By lunchtime, Trevor had grown fussy in spite of Megan's efforts. Unhappy about sitting in his stroller, he threw his baseball cap onto the ground time after time until Megan grew tired of his game.

'He's working on a new tooth,' she declared as she pulled a plastic teething ring filled with gel from the small insulated carrier she'd hung on one of the stroller handles. 'I'll be glad when it finally breaks through.'

She tried to hold him, but he refused to go to her. Instead, he arched his back and reached out to Jonas, in whose arms he'd been the happiest.

'Jonas is tired of carrying you,' she told the toddler. 'It's my turn.'

'I don't mind,' Jonas protested over Trevor's shrill voice.

'I do,' she said firmly. 'I didn't bring you along as a pack horse.'

Trevor wailed and, with a huge tear brimming in each eye, held out his arms toward Jonas. 'Dada,' he said plainly.

Jonas froze, his smile still in place. Angie squealed with delight. 'He talked.' She reached out and tickled his chin. 'You said a word. Good boy.'

'Oh, Jonas. Did you hear that? He finally said something we can understand.'

He'd heard all right. Loud and clear.

Dada. Daddy.

He didn't know why he felt as if he'd taken a blow to his midsection, but he did.

'Dada,' Trevor insisted.

'Jo-nas,' Megan enunciated.

'Dada.'

Jonas felt as if a noose were encircling his neck. 'Can you say Momma?'

Trevor looked him straight in the eye and said, 'Dada.'

'He's stuck,' Angie said importantly.

Megan laughed. 'Not for long. In a few more weeks, he'll probably say all kinds of things.'

'Dada!' Trevor shouted with vehemence, as if he was wondering why this man wasn't answering his call.

Jonas pulled himself out of his stupor and picked up the little boy who had quieted now that his wish had been granted. He knew both Angie and Trevor liked him, but had they started to think of him as a father? Until he'd heard the word 'dada' he hadn't thought of what leaving would do to them when they'd already lost so many important people in their young lives.

And now, because of his lack of foresight, they could well suffer again. If he didn't end things now, his departure would only create more pain for everyone, including himself.

That had been the whole purpose behind his rules. Keep

relationships light and don't attach strings of any kind. Now he would pay the price for ignoring his own advice.

Damn! He was in a mess with only one way out—one way to minimize the damage.

Megan laid a hand on his arm and a worried wrinkle appeared on her forehead. 'Are you OK?'

He focused his gaze on the distance rather than her face. 'Yeah.' He hoisted Trevor so that the toddler sat on his shoulders, high above the crowd.

Thirty minutes later Trevor said, 'Down,' and Megan declared an end to the day. 'Everyone's tired,' she told him.

Angie didn't argue, which only proved that Megan was right. 'Can we come again?' she asked.

Jonas let Megan field Angie's question. 'Of course.'

Angie tugged on his hand. 'Will you come with us, too?'

How could he answer? He knew what he had to do, but telling the little girl that he was walking out of their lives as quietly as he'd entered didn't seem the smart thing to do. She was too tired to fully understand and he wasn't ready for another scene.

He glanced at Megan, who simply stared at him with a raised eyebrow, as if she wanted to hear his response as well.

'We'll see,' he finally said.

Apparently mollified by his reply, Angie dropped the subject.

On the way home, Jonas remained silent, only interjecting a few comments when spoken to directly. The rest of the time he simply listened to Trevor babbling an occasional recognizable word and Angie describing everything she'd seen, from the monkeys swinging on the tree branches to the lions sleeping in the shade of their vine-covered canopy.

Megan sensed something was wrong. Jonas was far too quiet for a man who'd been bursting with enthusiasm a few hours earlier. She could pinpoint the exact moment he'd withdrawn—the moment Trevor had said, 'Dada.'

The look on Jonas's face had reflected his shock and for a few seconds pure, unadulterated terror.

She didn't need a Ph.D. after her name to know that Jonas was terrified. If he'd driven his own vehicle, he would probably have torn a strip off his tires in his haste to leave, but because they'd come together in her car, he was stuck.

She intended to take advantage of the situation, and while he drove through Stanton she mentally prepared her arguments for the upcoming battle. And it would be a battle—a battle for their future—because she knew as surely as she knew her own name that Jonas would put an end to what they had.

Covering her mouth with her hand as she stared out the window, Megan stifled a groan of pain. This had been the most marvelous week of her life, a week where she'd allowed herself to fantasize about a happy ending, and now the fantasy was fading before her eyes.

By the time he pulled into her driveway, Trevor was sound asleep and Angie not far behind.

'I'll help you carry them inside,' he said softly.

'Thanks.' She watched him hoist Angie to his shoulder with ease while she unbuckled Trevor. Watching Jonas carry the little girl like she was a precious treasure brought tears to her eyes.

Jonas had so much to offer a family. Why couldn't he see that?

Why *wouldn't* he see that?

She didn't want to lose him. She'd only put up a token resistance to Dwight's defection but, then, she hadn't loved him the way she loved Jonas. Determined to fight with everything she had, she carefully placed Trevor in his bed while Jonas did the same for Angie. Minutes later, she rejoined him in the living room.

'That was quite a day,' she said brightly.

'We need to talk.'

She nodded. 'I thought you'd say that.' *Oh, please, help me be convincing*, she thought as she sat on the sofa.

'This isn't going to work,' he began.

She'd known what was coming, but a part of her had hoped she'd misread his intent. Although she'd tried to prepare herself mentally, the blow still struck hard. If he wanted to run, she didn't intend to make it easy for him.

'Why not?'

'We wanted different things.'

'Did we? I don't know about you, but I wanted companionship and I thought that's what we had.'

'We did. We do, but…' He ran both hands over his head. 'Damn it, Megan. I'm not father material. Or husband material, for that matter.'

'Who says?'

'I do.'

'Well, you're wrong.' She scooted to the edge of the sofa. 'I've seen you with Trevor and Angie and I know how you are with me. You're kind, thoughtful, considerate. If those aren't qualities that any one would want in a spouse or a parent, I don't know what are.'

'Did you hear what Trevor called me?'

'Yes. He's obviously overheard some of Angie's conversations about mommies and daddies. It doesn't mean anything. If you recall, he called me dada, too.'

'The point is, they're getting attached to me and that won't work.'

'Are you worried about their attachment to you, or your attachment to them?'

He fell silent and she knew she'd pegged his fear correctly.

'They love you, Jonas, because you're sweet and kind and special. They sense that and probably always did.'

Jonas paced. 'I can't be what they need. I'm like one of those migratory birds we saw today. I can't stay in one place.'

'Can't? Or won't?' He didn't answer. 'Explain it to me, Jonas. I want to understand.'

'I don't want any ties.'

'Why not?' she pressed.

'Because it hurts to leave.'

'Then don't.'

'I have to.'

'Why?'

'Would you stop with the twenty questions?' he exploded.

Megan refused to back down. 'I will when you give me a good answer.'

He hesitated, as if considering her request and deciding what to say. 'I told you that we moved a lot.'

'Yes.'

'Well, I spent a lot of time with other families when my dad was gone. Some were OK, some weren't. There were two families that were special. They treated me like I was one of theirs and I made the mistake of pretending that I was. I was heartbroken when my dad was transferred, and after the second time I decided I couldn't go through that again.'

'You're not that child any longer, Jonas,' Megan said softly.

'No, but it wasn't too long ago when a med school friend of mine who positively doted on his wife and three kids lost everything. She decided that she didn't like raising a family by herself because he was gone more often than not, so she moved out. Harry was forced to rely on her good will in order to see his own children and, believe me, her good will came in short supply.'

'Didn't he have court-ordered visitation?'

He snorted. 'A lot of good that did. If she didn't want to let them see him, she made some excuse like the kids were sick or they were staying at a friend's house. I can't tell you how many times he was supposed to have them for the weekend and he'd end up at my place, getting drunk because she'd cancelled. The sad thing is that he would have been a marvelous pediatrician, but he couldn't handle being around other people's kids. He finally switched to orthopedics. I don't need that kind of heartache.'

How could she counter those sorts of experiences? Any one would leave emotional scars, but adding them together made for a deadly combination.

'No, you don't,' she agreed. 'But that doesn't mean your life will be a carbon copy of his.'

'No, but what I know about parenting or being a husband wouldn't fill the tip of an eyedropper.'

'So you do like everyone else. You learn as you go. It isn't a case of some people have this knowledge and others don't. We all have to pick up things by trial and error. We'll make mistakes, but as long as we try, what more can anyone ask?'

Jonas shook his head. 'I can't do it.'

Megan was running out of cards to play. 'So you're going to run.'

'It's better this way.'

'For whom? You? I can't believe you want to spend your life alone, like Violet Spears. If you think I'm better off without you, then guess again.' She drew a bracing breath and played her final card. 'I love you.'

He flinched as if he couldn't carry another burden on his shoulders. 'Don't make this harder than it already is.'

She straightened her spine. 'I'm not trying to be difficult. I only want you to know how I feel.'

'I warned you that I wasn't interested in anything permanent. You shouldn't have expected it.'

'I didn't. I'd hoped, wished and dreamed that we could have something long-lasting, but I never *expected* anything.' She managed a smile. 'I'm not a glutton for punishment.'

'For what it's worth,' he said slowly, 'if I chose someone to stay with, it would be you.'

Later, she would grasp his words as a consolation, but now she couldn't.

'If I wasn't so angry with you for being so stubborn,' she retorted, 'I'd be flattered. But I am, so I'm not. Do you know what your problem is?' Before he could answer, she told him. 'For a man who holds people's lives in his hand, you're scared.'

He raised his voice. 'Damn right I am. With medicine, there are certain laws of nature that we follow, certain rules about how the body works that can't be broken. With a relationship, there's nothing. No guide book, no instruction manual. You're on your own.'

He was so adamant that she knew her aspirations of a future with him were doomed. Her eyes burned with unshed tears, but she blinked them away. 'No, you're not,' she said quietly. 'It takes two people to make it a success or a failure.'

'After Dwight, how can you say that?'

'After Dwight, I *have* to say that. I obviously didn't meet some need that he had. Maybe if we'd talked about it, we could have worked out the problem, but we didn't. Just because we broke up, it didn't mean I swore off ever having a relationship again.'

She hadn't then, but she would now. Jonas didn't need to know that, however.

'I think it's best if I fade into the woodwork,' he said with conviction. 'I'm leaving soon anyway.'

She'd failed, but she wasn't going to grovel. She had some pride.

'You're probably right,' she said with a serenity that she didn't feel. 'I love you, but you don't love me back. That happens and I can accept it.'

Actually, she couldn't, but she didn't have much choice.

'Please, promise me, though, that somewhere down the line you'll let yourself love someone. Otherwise you're going to waste a huge portion of yourself until all that's left is a shell of who you could have been.'

Sensing she was about to choke on the emotion she'd suppressed, Megan rose. 'Now, if you don't mind, I have a few chores to do before Trevor wakes and demands my full attention.'

Refusing to watch him walk out of her life, she turned on one heel and hid in her bedroom until she heard the front door close. The quiet snick unleashed the floodgates, and as she hugged her pillow to her face to stifle her sobs, she whispered her goodbyes.

# CHAPTER ELEVEN

JONAS drove home feeling as distraught and heartbroken as the fifteen-year-old boy who, out of self-preservation, had vowed not to grow attached to the families he lived with.

How was he supposed to feel, what was he supposed to think? Being called daddy and informed that the woman who'd wiggled her way into his heart loved him was bound to send any man running for cover, especially one who didn't have relationships, only flings.

Normally he said his goodbyes and moved on without a backward glance. He drove away with pleasant memories, satisfaction in his gut and a healthy anticipation of what lay ahead.

Now, as he severed the ties that had entangled him so unexpectedly, emptiness filled his soul. Why did Megan have to fall in love with him? It only made things worse. Who would have guessed that trying to save Dwight Fleming from an unhappy relationship would have totally changed his own life? He should have known better than to break the rules he'd created to save himself heartache.

'I did what had to be done,' he told Penny some fifteen minutes later. 'It's best to just rip the bandage off in one swoop.'

Yet, as he scratched the retriever's ears, he realized that his problem just wasn't with Megan. He had another problem lying at his feet.

His house and yard suddenly closed in around him. Impulsively, he escaped from the dog who was a reminder of unwanted ties and the house that reeked of Megan's scent.

Hoping to find peace on the golf course, he drove there like a man on a mission.

Eighteen holes and five lost balls later, he'd convinced himself that he bore enough responsibility with his profession. Adding a wife, two kids and a dog to the mix was simply asking too much. He would fail.

Suddenly, seeing Megan nearly every day for the next two months seemed like a cruel punishment. Without giving himself time to reconsider, he called his superior, Martin Akers, who co-ordinated the physicians' schedules.

'How's MacGregor doing?' he asked as soon as he'd identified himself.

Martin laughed. 'What's wrong, Taylor? Have you gone through all the single women in Stanton so soon?'

'You could say that,' he replied. 'Is there any chance that MacGregor can take over his position before July first?'

'Are you that bored that you can't wait to get back in the fast lane?' Martin teased.

'I just think I can do more good someplace else,' he evaded.

'That may be, but I'll have to check with MacGregor and see. I hear that he and his wife are finally doing the traveling she's been begging for, so I don't know if he'll agree to cut short his leave of absence. I'll let you know.'

'Fair enough.'

Jonas disconnected the call, encouraged that he could put all this behind him sooner than originally anticipated. All he had to do now was to figure out what to do with Penny…and how to turn off his regrets.

Megan spent Sunday morning explaining to Angie that she probably wouldn't see Jonas as often as she used to.

In typical four-year-old fashion, she asked, 'Why?'

'Because he's going to be moving away in a few weeks and he needs to pack.'

'It didn't take me long to pack when I moved here,' she said.

'Jonas has more things than you do.' The excuse was weak, but Angie wouldn't suspect otherwise. His house had come fully furnished and, as far as Megan had been able to tell during her visits, he wasn't a man prone to collecting possessions.

Of course he wouldn't, she thought with exasperation. Those reminders of people and places would only form the very ties that he shunned.

'Why does he have to move?'

'Because it's part of his job.'

'Why can't his job let him stay here?'

'He has to work in other hospitals. *That's* his job.'

'Then he won't be our daddy, either?'

Megan stroked Angie's hair. 'When I find someone special to be your daddy, I'll let you know.'

Angie shrugged. 'Will he come back and visit us?'

Megan hugged Angie and swallowed the lump in her throat. She couldn't tell the truth. She simply couldn't. 'Some day.'

Although Angie took Megan's answer in her stride, Megan noticed that she started to wear her angel wings again.

Trevor was a different story. He toddled from room to room, calling for 'dada.' It broke her heart to watch him search for a man who wasn't there and never would be again.

'His name is Jonas,' she coaxed repeatedly. 'Jo-nas.'

Trevor would look up at her with a question in his big brown eyes. 'O-na?'

'Jonas,' Megan would say firmly.

'Dada,' came Trevor's reply. 'Dada.'

Hearing that word over and over strained Megan's stressed nerves, but what could she do? She'd prayed for the day when Trevor would finally talk. It wasn't his fault that his first and obviously favorite word was the one guaranteed to cause her pain.

*I hope you're happy, Jonas.*

On Monday morning, Trevor started bouts of inconsolable crying. Fortunately, Megan didn't have to take him to the hospital's child care center because it was her day off, so she did her best to draw his attention to his favorite toys and books. At times she was successful, but most often she wasn't.

By mid-afternoon, he would simply drop to the floor, draw his legs close to his body and whimper from what was obviously a severe stomach cramp. Her instincts warned her that this was more than feeling blue because Jonas hadn't appeared in answer to Trevor's call, but he didn't otherwise act like he had flu. What was even more puzzling was he acted perfectly fine, albeit pale, after each episode.

When she found his stool bloody and his abdomen swollen by late afternoon, her nurse's training shouted that this was definitely serious.

She discussed his symptoms with their pediatrician who advised her to bring him to his office immediately, although it was minutes before closing time. Without hesitation she dialed her mother to make arrangements for Angie.

'Can you watch her for a few hours?' she asked. 'Dr Bloomfield needs to see Trevor. Something's wrong.'

'Of course, dear,' Nancy told her after she described the situation. 'Why don't I drive over and save you the trip?'

'Thanks, Mom, but I'm ready to walk out of the door right now. We'll be there shortly.'

On the way to her parents', the mantle of single parenthood had never felt so heavy. She was tempted to call Jonas, to let his calm voice flow over her and settle her fears, but if she was going to cope with disasters and illness without him, she may as well start getting used to it now.

'Where are those lab reports?' Jonas barked at Louise. 'I can't believe it takes two hours to run a basic chemistry panel and a CBC.'

'I don't know.'

'Tell them if I don't have the results in five minutes, I'm filing a complaint. And I don't want some half-baked excuse either. I want to finish up this case so I can go home.'

'Yes, sir.' Louise eyed him warily as she picked up the phone.

Jonas stormed into his office. The day had been a continuation of his disastrous weekend and his mood hadn't improved since Saturday evening. No matter how many holes of golf he'd played, he simply hadn't found the peace he needed. A vision of Megan marrying someone else, Angie and Trevor smiling up at another man and calling him daddy, tormented him.

Yet he couldn't take the final step.

To make matters worse, he'd worried over seeing Megan for the first time since their little chat, and all for nothing. Because of the nurses' ten-hour shift schedules, she was off today.

The department should have run smoothly, but everything that could have gone wrong did. The computer system was down for two hours, the lab was slow, Radiology's CAT scanner went on the blink and Central Supply had run out of his glove size.

He paced back and forth. The entire ER staff had trodden softly around him today and he didn't blame them. He would have avoided himself if it had been possible.

The last forty-eight hours had been the longest and the

worst of his life. If he didn't work through this soon, the staff would boot him out the door long before MacGregor returned. Even the news that Violet Spears was recovering hadn't improved his temper.

Louise stood in the door with a piece of paper in hand. 'Here are those results.'

'It's about time.' He glanced over the form before handing it back to her. 'As soon as I discharge this patient, I'm out of here.'

She muttered something under her breath that sounded like 'Thank God', but he didn't respond. When he left some fifteen minutes later, he thought he heard a collective sigh in the background.

He'd take Penny for a run to blow the cobwebs out of his mind, he decided. Maybe more vigorous exercise would help his frame of mind. As he drove away from the hospital, he idly noticed a blue pickup following him, but his curiosity didn't grow until its driver parked in front of his house.

He climbed out of his vehicle and greeted Penny, who stood at the gate leading to the back yard with her nose pressed through the chain-link fence.

A man slid out of the truck and approached him. Jonas noted that he was in his thirties and wore obvious work clothes of jeans and a long-sleeved cotton shirt.

'Dr Taylor?' he asked.

Jonas rubbed Penny's head while he answered. 'Yes?'

'I'm Tom Billings. Dr Millard mentioned that you were interested in finding a home for your golden retriever.' He pointed to Penny. 'Is that her?'

'Yes, it is.' Jonas should have been thrilled by a prospective owner falling into his proverbial lap, but he wasn't. Even with Doug's apparent recommendation that this family would be suitable, he found himself hesitating. 'So you're looking for a dog?'

'My wife and I decided our son is old enough to look after a pet. We wanted an animal who's good with kids because Timmy is ten, Molly is eight and Meredith is four. Dr Millard suggested your dog might be what we need. Our place covers five acres, so she would have plenty of room to roam.'

'I see.'

This was what Jonas had wanted. It was the last tie that had to be severed. Yet as he stared at Penny's pleading eyes, his plan didn't seem quite as satisfying. The Billingses would take good care of Penny, he had no doubt. Penny would have plenty of space, get lots of exercise and have children loving her to death.

Sending Penny with him was for the best, but it was a jolt to realize that a mere ten-year-old boy was willing to do what a thirty-four-year-old man was not. And yet if he wasn't interested, why was he dragging his feet?

Penny whined and licked his fingers.

*Don't you want someone to talk to?* Megan's voice reverberated through his head. Penny had listened to him for hours these past two days. She was a darned sight cheaper than a therapist.

*Promise me that you'll let yourself love someone.*

Suddenly Jonas realized that he couldn't give up Penny. The retriever probably wasn't what Megan had had in mind when she'd shared her piece of advice, but for him it was a start. And wherever he went, Penny would be his link to Stanton...and to Megan.

'I'm sorry,' he said, 'but I've decided to keep her.'

In that instant, he also realized something else, something critical, something that would change his entire life.

He couldn't walk away from Megan either.

Instruction manual or not, he'd never be able to survive without her because his feelings went far deeper than he'd ever imagined. He loved her.

No wonder he felt as if he'd ripped out his heart because, in essence, he had. He *loved* her, and that knowledge made the tightness in his chest ease. For the first time in thirty-six hours, he could breathe without pain.

The man nodded. 'I can see where she'd be a hard one to let go. If you should change your mind, I'm in the phone book.'

'Thanks for stopping by,' Jonas told him, knowing that, no matter what, he wouldn't call Tom Billings.

Eager to talk to Megan, he quickly changed into more comfortable clothes while Penny ate her dinner. The emptiness inside him had completely disappeared. He might not have initially embraced the idea of being a husband and father, but now he couldn't imagine going back to his previous way of life.

He'd made the right decision.

As soon as Penny was ready for her evening walk, they set out and traveled the distance in record time. He half expected to meet Angie on her trike with her wings flying and wheels squeaking as Megan and Trevor followed, but he didn't.

Anticipation turned to bewilderment when he saw their house was quiet and dark. Even her mini-van was missing from its usual spot on the driveway.

Disappointed that he'd have to wait to talk to her, he let Penny run off her excess energy. Their route took them through another residential zone, a playground and past the hospital. By chance, he noticed Megan's vehicle in the parking lot and its presence worried him.

Had something happened to her father? He couldn't leave without knowing, so he tied Penny's leash to the bench near the entrance and went inside. Because all admissions came through the emergency room after six, he knew the staff there could give him some answers.

He stopped Rick, his evening shift counterpart. 'I saw

Megan Erickson's car outside. I was wondering if her father had hurt himself.'

Rick shook his head. At fifty-five, he preferred the slower pace of small-town hospitals. 'It's her little boy. They're in Radiology.'

His heart skipped a beat. 'Trevor? What's wrong with him?'

If anything had happened...

'Bloomfield ordered barium studies. That's all I know.'

Jonas didn't hesitate. He made a beeline for Radiology, pausing only to say, 'In case anyone asks, the dog tethered outside is mine.'

He strode down the hall, peering into each X-ray suite until he saw Megan sitting on one of the uncomfortably hard plastic chairs for waiting patients. Apparently exhausted from his ordeal, Trevor lay against her, his head tucked in the crook of her neck, his eyes closed and with a stuffed white rabbit clutched in one small fist.

The sight roused Jonas's protective instincts and strengthened his resolve to put his relationship with Megan to rights. He wanted to claim her and her family as his.

'I saw your car in the lot.' He spoke softly so as not to disturb the sleeping toddler. 'Rick told me you were here.'

Megan stared down the hall. 'You shouldn't have come.'

Her flat tone bothered him. 'I had to know what was going on.'

'I don't want you here.'

'I understand you're still hurt and angry, but I have to tell you—'

'I'm not in the mood to rehash our previous discussion. Please, leave before Trevor wakes. It confuses him if you pop in and out of his life at your whim, like a jack-in-the-box.'

She was clearly at breaking point and it bothered him to know how he'd contributed to her state of mind. If only he'd come to his senses before he'd broken her spirit. He deserved every harsh word, and more.

'I'll go,' he promised, vowing her reprieve would only be temporary, 'as soon as you tell me what's wrong with Trevor.'

She recited his symptoms in a monotone. 'He started having abdominal cramps this morning and by this afternoon his stools were bloody. I called Dr Bloomfield before his office closed and as soon as he'd examined Trevor he sent us here for tests. The X-ray showed an intestinal blockage and the follow-up ultrasound showed an intussusception.'

The condition she'd mentioned was both rare and dangerous in young children. For reasons not quite understood, a portion of the intestine folded in on itself. If the problem wasn't rapidly diagnosed, the tissues around the bowel that contained the blood vessels got trapped and strangulated. The resultant swelling only made the situation worse until finally the section of intestine died. The key to a successful outcome was early diagnosis.

'So what's next? Surgery?'

She shook her head. 'Dr Bloomfield said it didn't appear that there was much swelling. He wanted to do a barium enema in the hope that the pressure of the fluid flowing through the intestine would force out the portion that had telescoped on itself.'

Jonas knew that if the enema didn't reduce or pop out the intussusception, surgery would be the next step. Before he could encourage her, Dr Bloomfield, Stanton's fifty-eight-year-old white-haired pediatrician, rounded the corner.

'Have they started taking pictures on our boy?'

'We finished about ten minutes ago.'

'Good, good,' Bloomfield said in his deep voice. He looked at Jonas. 'Has she told you the situation?'

He nodded. 'Then you think the barium will do the trick?'

'I'm hopeful. We'll find out after we look at the films.' He patted Megan's arm. 'One way or another, he'll be fixed up by morning.'

Megan nodded, although Jonas could see the worry on her face. He wanted to hold her hand, but he doubted if she'd let him.

'I'll be back shortly.' Bloomfield glanced at Jonas. 'Have you seen many cases?'

'A few,' he admitted.

'Good, then you know what we need to look for.'

It was as close to an invitation for a consult as he had ever heard. Jonas debated leaving Megan, but the grim set to her mouth suggested that she wanted him out of sight and out of mind.

'Is it OK with you?' he asked warily.

She sounded too tired to protest. 'Suit yourself.'

He gratefully went with Bloomfield who patiently waited as the radiology tech fixed the series of films to the view-box. 'Statistics indicate the barium usually resolves the problem in children, but I can't say I've observed that in my practice.'

'Neither have I,' Jonas admitted, although he didn't expect his experiences to match Bloomfield's. Jonas usually treated adults because large city hospitals often staffed their emergency rooms with a pediatrician. His pediatrics experience was usually limited to small facilities such as Stanton's.

'On the other hand, I usually don't see the kids until their symptoms are more advanced.' Bloomfield pointed to the narrowed spot that Jonas's sharp eye had also noticed. 'Well, now, lookee here.'

'That's it.'

As soon as they came to the last picture in the series, Jonas grinned.

Bloomfield sounded completely satisfied. 'What did I tell you? The barium pushed it back out.'

'I've never seen it happen before. My cases always required surgery.'

'It's all in early diagnosis. Thank goodness Megan was alert and didn't wait for him to get better on his own. Shall we tell her the good news?'

Jonas accompanied the pediatrician to where they'd left Megan and Trevor. Neither had moved and Megan looked up at their approach. Lines of dread and worry etched her face as she clutched Trevor to her.

Although Jonas intended the older physician to explain, he bestowed his widest smile on her. As she gazed at him, the fear on her face slowly turned to cautious optimism.

'He's a lucky boy,' Bloomfield said. 'The enema fixed the problem.'

'Are you sure?'

Trevor stirred in her tight embrace. His eyelids popped open and he raised his head off her shoulder. His lower lip quivered as his gaze landed on Dr Bloomfield, but before he could bury his face in Megan's neck again, Jonas caught his attention.

'Hi, big guy,' he said.

Trevor immediately brightened. He raised his head to say, 'Dada.' This time, the name didn't bother Jonas in the slightest. He hoped to hear it often.

'He'll probably sleep well tonight,' Bloomfield said. 'A small percentage of cases have recurrences, so watch him closely for a while.'

'I will.'

'Then I'll leave you folks to go home and put this fella to bed.'

Jonas helped Megan gather up Trevor's things, determined to stick close for as long as possible.

'I can't believe he'll be fine,' she said as she juggled Trevor and her purse. 'I was so afraid he'd need surgery.'

'He was lucky.' He hoisted Trevor's bag to his shoulder.

'I can carry that,' she said, reaching for it.

He gripped it tightly. 'I'll take it to the car for you.'

Now that he was feeling better and going home, Trevor chattered nonsense to anyone who would listen. Outside, as Jonas untied Penny's leash and they started toward her mini-van, the youngster said, 'Dog.'

'That's right,' Megan replied. 'Penny's a dog.'

'Wa'?' he asked.

Instinctively, Jonas knew what he wanted. 'No, we're not taking Penny for a walk. It's bedtime.'

'We're going bye-bye,' Megan said. 'Tell Jonas bye-bye.'

Trevor waved before she buckled him into his car seat.

A moment later, she straightened and headed for the driver's door. 'Goodbye, Jonas.'

He stalled for time. 'Where's Angie?'

'At my mother's. I'm on my way to pick her up.'

'Why don't I?' he asked. 'After I take Penny home, I have to run to the store near your parents' complex. You can put Trevor to bed and relax.'

She heaved a sigh. 'Why are you being nice? It would be easier if you weren't.'

He grinned. 'It's my roguish personality.' At her hesitation, he added, 'Please? I really want to do this.'

'Fine.' She sounded exasperated. 'I'll call Mom and tell her you're coming.'

'I'll be there in thirty minutes.'

Determined not to waste any time, he hurried home. As soon as he'd settled Penny in the back yard, he made one phone call to put his plan in motion, then showered before driving to the store for the item he'd requested.

The lady in the jewelry department delivered her goods as promised. He paid for his purchase, then went to collect Angie.

She met him at the door, wearing her nightgown and fuzzy pink slippers. 'Mommy called and said Trevor's better.'

'That's right,' he said. 'Do you have everything?'

She nodded as her grandmother smiled down to her benevolently. 'I'd ask you to stay and visit,' Nancy said, 'but it's past Angie's bedtime.'

'I'll be back soon,' he promised. 'With Megan.'

She studied him carefully before her intent gaze softened as if she had read his unspoken message. 'Dean and I will look forward to it.'

During the drive home, Angie wanted to hear about Trevor, so Jonas patiently explained it in four-year-old terms. By the time he'd finished he was parking behind Megan's mini-van and Angie was yawning.

The porch light was on and the open door welcoming as he carried Angie up the steps. Earlier, he'd been afraid that Megan would refuse to let him inside, but he'd managed to circumvent that hurdle. Now he only hoped that the item in his pocket would convince her of his change of heart.

Megan covered Trevor with his favorite blanket before she patted his back and kissed his temple. 'Sweet dreams,' she murmured.

Satisfied that he was fully asleep, she tiptoed from the room. She wanted desperately to collapse into bed, but she still had one more trial to endure.

Why Jonas had bothered to check on her at the hospital was a complete mystery. He'd broken the tenuous ties between them on Saturday and it made no sense for him to walk back into her life.

She simply wouldn't allow it. One goodbye was enough. She refused to suffer through another.

She should have refused his offer to bring Angie home, but she hadn't been able to summon the energy to fight him on such a trivial point. Sheer determination had been the only thing holding her together at the time, but now, with Trevor in bed and fresh resolve in her heart, she'd show him the door and try not to close it on his behind when he left.

Standing in the living room, she heard a car door slam and knew he had arrived. Squaring her shoulders and telling herself to stand firm, she greeted him as he walked inside.

'She's asleep,' he told her. 'Is her bed ready?'

Megan led the way to Angie's room and turned down the sheets. It gave her an odd sensation to watch Jonas place her daughter on the mattress, remove her slippers and gently stroke her hair before he covered her with the comforter. His action was too touching for her to watch without tears filling her eyes, so she turned and left.

He joined her a minute later in the living room, but she didn't give him a chance to speak.

'Thanks for bringing Angie home. Goodnight, Jonas.'

'We need to talk.'

'There's nothing to be said.'

'I think there is.' He dug in his pocket and removed a small, flat box, about the size of a necklace. 'I want to show you this.'

Instant suspicion flared. 'What is it?'

'Go ahead. Open it.'

Reluctantly, she did as he urged. Nestled inside on a bed of cotton lay a large dog tag in the shape of a bone.

'Read the engraving.'

Megan lifted it out and turned it so the light fell on the

words. 'My name is Penny and I belong to J. Taylor and family.' She looked at him, bewildered. 'The address is mine.'

'I hope you don't mind. I figure Penny and I will spend most of our time over here anyway.'

'But, Jonas—'

'This tag is only temporary until I can order one from the vet.'

'But—'

'Don't talk. Just listen.'

She obeyed because she was too surprised to do anything else.

'I've been miserable without you, but I didn't understand why until tonight when a man came by who wanted Penny. I realized that I couldn't let her go because I've grown attached to her.'

Megan found her voice. 'What about your argument of how difficult it is to move a dog around the country?'

He continued as if she hadn't interrupted. 'At the same time, I realized that I couldn't let you go either.'

Tears burned her eyes, but she didn't know if they were happy tears or just a sign that the day's stresses had been too much.

He stepped close to touch her cheek. 'I love you, Megan. I don't know what kind of husband or father I'll make, but I want to try.'

She could hardly believe that he was saying the words she'd longed to hear. 'Are you serious?'

'Never more so.'

Clutching the dog tag like a talisman, she flung her arms around his neck and smiled through her tears. 'Oh, Jonas.'

He grinned. 'I assume you're happy?'

'Deliriously.' A thought occurred to her. 'But what about your job?'

'I don't have that detail worked out yet,' he admitted.

'I'm slated to cover a hospital in Wyoming, which will make for a long commute for a while. While I'm there, I'll hunt for a position that will keep me in one place, preferably one around here so you can stay near your parents.'

Megan was overwhelmed by his thoughtfulness. 'They'll appreciate it so much.'

'I thought they might.'

'Angie will be so excited when she hears the news. Poor Trevor walked through the house all weekend, calling for "Dada".'

'We could always wake them.'

'Absolutely not,' she protested, horrified at the thought. 'Tomorrow will be soon enough. Tonight is ours.'

A grin slowly spread across his face. 'I do like the way you think.'

# EPILOGUE

SERENA and Bonnie adjusted Megan's wedding veil as she waited in the vestibule of Stanton's Holy Family Church with Angie and her father as they waited for the signal to begin.

'You're such a beautiful bride,' Bonnie sniffled. 'Wouldn't you know it? There isn't a single place on this dress to hide a tissue.'

Megan had chosen form-fitting forest-green dresses with halter necklines for Serena and Bonnie to wear as her attendants. Serena was blonde, like Bonnie, and the dark color looked good on both of them. Angie, as flower girl, wore the same color, but in a princess-style gown identical to Megan's.

'Bride, heck. Did you get a look at her groom?' Serena teased. 'Aw sweetie, you two are going to be a great couple.'

'Thanks. I think so, too.'

'I can't believe Jonas chose Dwight as his best man,' Serena said.

'It seemed appropriate. He was responsible for bringing us together,' Megan reminded her.

'Yeah, well, I wonder if he wishes otherwise.'

Megan smiled. On occasion, when Dwight had run into their small family, she'd seen the look of regret and longing on his face, but she knew his decision has been the best for all of them. Someday, Dwight would find the right woman.

'Anyway,' Serena said, 'his loss is Jonas's gain.'

A familiar high-pitched voice shouted, 'Dada', and Megan knew that her future husband and the minister had entered the sanctuary.

Bonnie giggled. 'Trevor certainly has a powerful set of lungs.'

Megan's father gave up his position near the door where he'd waited for the minister's signal. The music changed to the entrance song Megan had chosen.

'It's time,' he said, his eyes bright.

Angie ambled down the long aisle first, followed by Bonnie, then Serena. Megan threaded her arm through her father's and drew a deep breath.

'Are you ready?' he asked, smiling benevolently on her.

In the distance, she could see Jonas standing tall and looking exceptionally handsome in his black tuxedo. 'Yes, Daddy. I am.'

She started down the aisle, pleased that her father was able to take this walk with her. The DBS that Jonas had suggested six months ago had drastically improved her father's condition. Although he still took medication, the dosages had been drastically reduced, and with therapy he'd regained a lot of the ground he'd lost.

Violet Spears sat in the crowd, looking clean and neat. Jonas had taken her under his wing and she considered herself to be Angie's and Trevor's second grandma. Megan didn't mind. What child could have too many grandparents?

Her gaze homed in on Jonas. She still didn't know how he'd managed it, but after a stint in Wyoming, which had been bearable because she'd arranged her off-duty time to coincide with his for those four months, he was in Stanton to stay. Somehow he'd convinced the hospital to hire him directly rather than through an agency, but she wasn't surprised. If he could talk Violet into moving into a retirement village, he could talk anyone into anything.

Right now, all she wanted to hear him say were the words that would make them husband and wife, and a family of four.

LIVE THE EMOTION

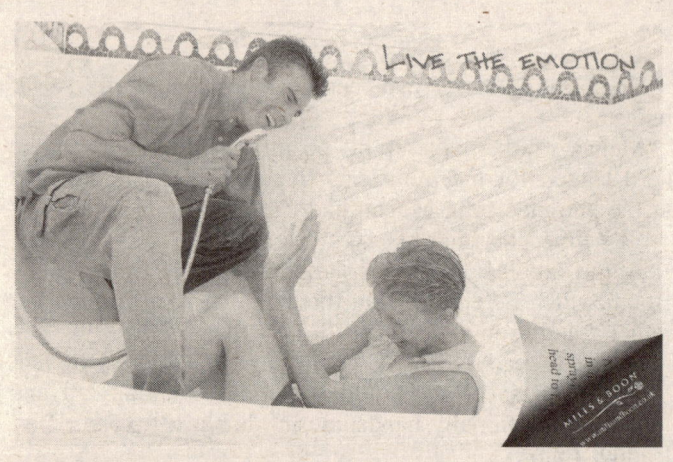

**Modern Romance**™
...seduction and passion guaranteed

**Tender Romance**™
...love affairs that last a lifetime

**Medical Romance**™
...medical drama on the pulse

**Historical Romance**™
...rich, vivid and passionate

**Sensual Romance**™
...sassy, sexy and seductive

*Blaze Romance*™
...the temperature's rising

*27 new titles every month.*

Live the emotion

MILLS & BOON®

MB3

# MILLS & BOON

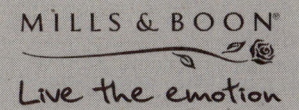

*Live the emotion*

# Medical Romance™

### A VERY SPECIAL MARRIAGE by *Jennifer Taylor*

Nurse Sophie Patterson was looking forward to a fresh start as resident nurse on board a luxury liner bound for the Mediterranean – until she discovered that her boss was Dr Liam Kennedy, her ex-husband! Her desire for him is brought back into stark reality, and Sophie's immediate response is to run. But Liam has realised he'll never love anyone as much as her – can he persuade her to stay…?

### THE ELUSIVE CONSULTANT by *Carol Marinelli*

Emergency charge nurse Tessa Hardy is stunned to discover that Max Slater is moving to England – without his fiancée! Tess is secretly in love with Max, though she knows she can't admit her feelings. Yet during a daring rescue operation Max stuns her by passionately kissing her – is this elusive consultant ready to be tamed? (*A&E Drama* miniseries)

### ENGLISHMAN AT DINGO CREEK by *Lucy Clark*

Dr Dannyella Thompson certainly needed help in her Outback practice – but an English doctor? She thought he'd be more amusement than assistance. But Dr Sebastian MacKenzie proved her wrong at every turn, and by the time his stay was up he'd won her over – in every way! Except to convince her that she should return to England with him as his bride… (*Doctors Down Under* miniseries)

## On sale 5th September 2003

*Available at most branches of WHSmith, Tesco, Martins, Borders, Eason, Sainsbury's and all good paperback bookshops.*

# MILLS & BOON

*Live the emotion*

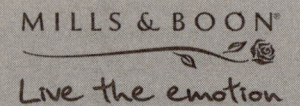

# Medical Romance™

### THE FRENCH SURGEON'S SECRET CHILD
*by Margaret Barker*

After one forbidden night, five years ago, Dr Liz Fitzgerald and surgeon Jacques Chenon decided never to see each other again. But now they're working together, and Jacques is everything Liz remembers – and more! He wants to rekindle every wonderful moment they had, but first Liz must tell him the truth about her four-year-old daughter… (*Mediterranean Doctors* miniseries)

### THE ITALIAN DOCTOR'S WIFE *by Sarah Morgan*

Children's heart surgeon Nico Santini has everything – intelligence, wealth, looks and talent. Who wouldn't want him to father her child? But Nurse Abby Harrington is horrified when he tells her that *he's* the father of her daughter – born via donor insemination. Nico is now unable to have children and Baby Rosa is his last chance.

### MIDWIFE IN NEED *by Fiona McArthur*

Midwife Abbey Wilson lives for her job and her family. But when Dr Rohan Roberts arrives at the maternity clinic in Gladstone, New South Wales, she becomes aware of a man for the first time in years. Abbey arouses all Rohan's desires and protective instincts, and he soon discovers his feelings for her are far deeper than he bargained for!

## On sale 5th September 2003

*Available at most branches of WHSmith, Tesco, Martins, Borders, Eason, Sainsbury's and all good paperback bookshops.*

# Invitations to Seduction

THREE SIZZLING STORIES FROM TODAY'S HOTTEST WRITERS!

VICKI LEWIS THOMPSON
CARLY PHILLIPS · JANELLE DENISON

**Available from 15th August 2003**

*Available at most branches of WH Smith,
Tesco, Martins, Borders, Eason, Sainsbury's
and all good paperback bookshops.*

# FREE!

## 4 Books
### and a surprise gift!

We would like to take this opportunity to thank you for reading this Mills & Boon® book by offering you the chance to take FOUR more specially selected titles from the Medical Romance™ series absolutely FREE! We're also making this offer to introduce you to the benefits of the Reader Service™—

- ★ FREE home delivery
- ★ FREE gifts and competitions
- ★ FREE monthly Newsletter
- ★ Books available before they're in the shops
- ★ Exclusive Reader Service discount

Accepting these FREE books and gift places you under no obligation to buy; you may cancel at any time, even after receiving your free shipment. Simply complete your details below and return the entire page to the address below. *You don't even need a stamp!*

**YES!** Please send me 4 free Medical Romance books and a surprise gift. I understand that unless you hear from me, I will receive 6 superb new titles every month for just £2.60 each, postage and packing free. I am under no obligation to purchase any books and may cancel my subscription at any time. The free books and gift will be mine to keep in any case.

M3ZEF

Ms/Mrs/Miss/Mr ............................................................Initials ................................
BLOCK CAPITALS PLEASE

Surname..................................................................................................................

Address..................................................................................................................

..............................................................................................................................

..........................................................................................Postcode ....................

**Send this whole page to:**
**UK: The Reader Service, FREEPOST CN81, Croydon, CR9 3WZ**
**EIRE: The Reader Service, PO Box 4546, Kilcock, County Kildare (stamp required)**

Offer not valid to current Reader Service subscribers to this series. We reserve the right to refuse an application and applicants must be aged 18 years or over. Only one application per household. Terms and prices subject to change without notice. Offer expires 28th November 2003. As a result of this application, you may receive offers from Harlequin Mills & Boon and other carefully selected companies. If you would prefer not to share in this opportunity please write to The Data Manager at the address above.

Mills & Boon® is a registered trademark owned by Harlequin Mills & Boon Limited.
Medical Romance™ is being used as a trademark.